FRAME-UP

by

Andrew Garve [, PSEUD.

Paul Winterton

HARPER & ROW, PUBLISHERS

NEW YORK AND EVANSTON

FRAME-UP

1

On a murky Sunday evening in November, John Lumsden stood in the studio of his Radlett home with a glass of dry sherry in his hand, regarding from a little distance a chessboard with a few pieces set out on it. His stance was slightly self-conscious—though there was no one around to see him. His interest in the board was something of a pose, too, for he was rarely able to solve these chess problems from the *Guardian* on his own. But he liked to feel he was the sort of man who tried.

Standing there, with his glass poised and his head on one side, he made a rather quaint figure. He was an elderly man of small stature—scarcely more than five foot four—with a wrinkled face and neck. He had a gray, close-cropped mustache, an affectation dating back to World War II. A pointed gray beard, of more recent growth, covered a weak, pointed chin. A few sparse hairs carefully arranged above his high forehead failed to conceal the essential baldness of his scalp. His eyes were alert and intelligent, with crow's-feet of humor at the corners. He was far from being an impressive man, but he looked a well-disposed one. He was wearing a wine-colored sweater, silver-gray slacks, and maroon slippers. He could have been a retired don enjoying a quiet evening—but in fact he was an artist.

He abandoned the chess problem very soon and started to walk up and down the studio, with short, jaunty steps. It was a large room, more than thirty-five feet long, with a working part and a living part. At the north end, under a big window now covered by a blind, was his easel with an unfinished painting on it, his palette and brushes and paints, his overalls on a hook, his stacked canvases, his sketchbook—all the tools of what he liked to call his trade. At the opposite end were three easy chairs placed round a fire, an antique desk of fine workmanship with a telephone and a framed photograph of a woman on it, a bureau of the same period, and a sixteenth-century Italian cabinet of which Lumsden was extremely proud. The walls of the room were lined with pictures, mostly of his own painting.

He hummed as he strutted, for he was in a genial humor. He had had no trace all day of the nervous indigestion that so often troubled him—which he took to be a good sign for the future. It was a pity that on this rather special Sunday night George hadn't been able to come—they'd have had a particularly convivial meal. . . . But he didn't mind eating alone for once—and Kathie, his housekeeper, would be back at nine thirty. He could rely on that. He was really a most fortunate man. And she was undeniably a fortunate woman. He paused for a moment beside the cabinet, fingering its embossed decorations, smiling with secret satisfaction at the thought of its contents. . . . He paused again by the picture on the easel, looking at it appraisingly. He didn't think it was too bad. Anyway, George had thought it was shaping up nicely. He took a few more turns. . . . A pleasant place, this studio—warm but airy, spacious enough for a bit of exercise. Walking here, he felt like an admiral pacing his quarterdeck.

A clock struck outside and he glanced at his watch. Half past seven. Fine!—he was ready for his meal. First, though, his all-purpose vitamin tablet. He shook one out from the bottle on his desk and swallowed it. Then he crossed to the little table, where Kathie had laid out supper for him. Cold turkey and salad, a piece of ripe Stilton, and half a bottle of Beaune. Very nice, too! He noticed that the wineglass beside the bottle had some tiny fragments of fluff sticking to it, from the cloth that Kathie had used to wipe it. He took it into the kitchen and got himself a clean one, with an indulgent smile.

He folded the *Observer* at an article pleading for the preservation of Venice, poured some wine, and sat down to enjoy his supper. He'd barely begun when he heard footsteps coming up the front drive. Now who could that be . . . ?

2

A little after nine o'clock that evening, Kathie Bowen left her sister's home in Hendon to drive back to Radlett in John Lumsden's Rover car. She was small and slender, with a good figure for her age—which was thirty-eight. Generally, she contrived to look younger. All traces of gray had been tinted out of her dark and wavy hair. Hard dieting had thinned her face, revealing good bones. The long Irish lashes that fringed her green eyes were discreetly emphasized. All her make-up was carefully applied. Keeping herself attractive was a task that occupied much of Kathie's time and attention.

Tonight, though, she had more important things to think of than her appearance. Her expression, as she drove off, suggested a deep inner turmoil. She was, in fact, both scared and exhilarated. Scared, because of the risk she was running, because of the finality of what she'd agreed to—and because she had more qualms about it than

either Eileen or Frank. . . . Exhilarated, because of what it offered.
. . . The comfort of the luxurious car and the enveloping coziness
of the fur coat John Lumsden had given her were just a foretaste of
the things she could look forward to from now on, if all went well.
Things that were going to make the future really worth while for
her—and for Eileen and Frank, too.

She accelerated up a steep rise, enjoying the silent power of the
car just as Frank had done. No more worries, she thought, about
whether she could afford this or that. No more anxieties about what
would happen to her as she got older. Financial security was almost
within her grasp. Now she'd be able to indulge herself a bit—and
why not? It was something that every woman wanted to do. . . .
Now she'd be able to buy all the clothes that took her fancy, without bothering about the price; to have a fine, comfortable home of
her own; to travel to the places she'd always dreamt of, the gay,
sunny places. . . . A marvelous prospect . . .

Not, she reflected, that she'd had a miserable time during the
fifteen years since Arthur's death. Far from it. She'd always believed in taking what she could get from life—and she'd probably
enjoyed herself as much as most people did. She'd been quite a
merry widow, really. But there'd been no feeling of permanence
about anything. No permanence about the jobs she'd done—looking after other people's households, without ever having a place of
her own. No permanence about the affairs she'd had—only a tran-
sient satisfaction and an ache for something better. Which never
came . . . And always the feeling of dependence, of not having any
real status . . .

It wasn't as though she hadn't tried desperately hard to change
things. She'd really worked on that stockbroker at Leatherhead,
who'd been handsome as well as rich. She'd done everything she
could to please him. She'd made a terrific effort to improve her
cooking for him. She'd coped with most of the housework, because
he hadn't wanted anyone else living in. She'd always dressed well
when he was around—better than she could really afford. She'd
tried to be entertaining and intelligent—even when she hadn't felt
like it. She'd dieted madly to keep slim. And where had it all got
her? Nowhere! It had all been wasted effort—he just hadn't come

up to scratch. Perhaps because she'd tried *too* hard. Or perhaps because, even then, she'd seemed too old. Marrying again was fine in theory—but first you had to be asked. . . .

Well, that episode was deep in the past now. Not forgotten— remembered, rather, as a useful lesson. The stockbroker would be her last failure, her last humiliation. Now she had grown really tough. She knew what she wanted, and she knew just how she was going to get it. It meant taking a huge gamble—but so did every- thing that was worth having. That was her view, anyway—and Eileen and Frank had agreed with her, had enthusiastically taken up the plan. . . .

In any case, it was done now. . . .

The clock in the tower of Stone Cross Hospital struck nine thirty as she turned the car into Wilton Crescent, where Lumsden lived. Right on time, she thought. She peered ahead, looking for the en- trance to the drive through the wiped segment of the windshield. . . . It was a horrible night—not really foggy, but raw, with a wet mist. Probably that was why the Crescent was so quiet—usually there was rather a lot of coming and going on a Sunday evening. A nice place to live, the Crescent. Lovely houses, modern and easy to run and not too big—all secluded in their own fine gardens, away from the noises of the road. Just the sort of place she'd have chosen for herself, if she'd been asked to make the choice. Perhaps with a little flat in the West End as well, for the odd night. And a white villa on the Costa del Sol, for the winter . . . Oranges and bougain- villea . . . Well, who could tell . . . ?

She could make out the lights of the house now, dim through the mist and the fringe of trees. She felt tense—and a little queasy. She must pull herself together—this, after all, was only the begin- ning. She turned the car through the white gate posts and garaged it and walked to the front door and let herself in with her key. In the hall, she stood for a moment, listening. The house was quiet. She hung up her outdoor clothes and went through into the studio. . . .

On the threshold she stopped, rooted by sudden panic. The room was in chaos. A chair was lying on its side, there was broken glass on the parquet floor, the telephone receiver was dangling on its cord. . . . She forced herself to go forward into the room. On the floor, beside the desk, John Lumsden lay sprawled, face downward, motionless. . . .

3

The studio was full of policemen. One of them had a camera and was taking flashbulb pictures of the scene—the body from all angles, the overturned chair, the chessboard, the scarcely touched meal, the photograph frame on the floor which was apparently the source of the broken glass. Another man, dusting for fingerprints, was cautiously examining a larger fragment of the glass which he'd found on the top of the desk. A police doctor was bent over the black and swollen face of the dead man. A uniformed constable stood by.

The man in charge of all the operations was Chief Inspector Charles Grant, of the C.I.D., Scotland Yard. In normal circumstances a murder case in Radlett would have been handled in the first instance by the Hertfordshire force, but it happened that three of their senior detectives were out of action and the Yard was temporarily covering for them. Grant had arrived a few minutes ago. He was a tall, lithe man of forty—smooth-faced and sleek, with the long eager nose of a greyhound and a thin sardonic mouth. Criminals usually found his expression most unpleasant. His colleagues at the Yard knew it as a cultivated professional front and disregarded it. There were jocular detectives, and grim detectives, and bullying detectives, and detectives who looked as though they'd just noticed a bad smell. Grant was one of these.

He was at the phone now, holding the receiver delicately because of the prints that were on it, talking to the operator. "It's the police here," he said. "The receiver of this telephone has been off for a while—I'd like to know more about it. . . . All right, put me through. . . ."

He waited, his eyes on the body. A very small man, John Lumsden, he thought. Surprising, really, that the room was in such a state. A puny man . . . A bit grotesque, too. Unfair to judge him now, of course—but he couldn't have been very prepossessing, even in life. Not exactly one's idea of an artist, either, in spite of the beard. But Grant knew, better than most, that you couldn't go by appearances. . . .

A voice cut into his thoughts—brisk, authoritative. "Can I help you?"

"Ah, Supervisor—this is the police—Chief Inspector Grant. I'm investigating a murder. . . . Yes . . . This telephone receiver has been off for some time. . . . Oh, you do . . . ? I see. . . . A woman . . . ? When did you get this inquiry? *Exactly* at ten minutes to eight . . . ? Good—I'd like to have that note. . . . Yes, I'll get someone to collect it. . . . Continuous engaged signal—yes, of course. . . . And the inquiry came from . . . ? Flaxman 0 0 six seven . . . Right . . . May I have your name, please . . . ? Mullins . . . Thank you, Supervisor."

Grant put the receiver back carefully and jotted the number down in his notebook. For a moment he stood eyeing the little heap of personal effects that had been removed from the dead man's pockets. A bunch of keys, a handkerchief, some loose change, and a notecase from the hip containing fifteen pounds. . . . That seemed to settle one thing, anyhow—the murderer hadn't been after cash. What about entry? Grant left the studio and inspected the front and back doors of the house. Both had self-closing latches and neither showed any sign of damage. He went on round the house, examining the downstairs windows and their fastenings. They were all intact. So this hadn't been the common sort of crime—violence by some tough who'd broken in to see what he could get. Grant's interest in the case began to rise. He could take the sordid brutality of the underworld in his stride as well as the next man, but it was the rare puzzle that, professionally speaking, he always hoped for. And this was certainly an intriguing start.

He went outside, shining his flashlight around to see if the murderer had left any helpful marks. The drive had a gravel surface, too loose to take any impressions. He examined the flower beds and the lawns, glistening with moisture, but found nothing. He walked slowly round to the back of the house. There were more lawns there, flanked by thick shrubberies. Between the lawns, a paved path led down to a wooden gate at the bottom of the garden. The gate had no lock and Grant went through it into another, public path which, after a few yards, joined a road. A quiet way to the house, he thought—but when he examined the garden path more closely he saw that no one had used it for some time. It was mossy and damp and would certainly have shown footmarks—but the only marks were Grant's own. And the grass at the sides looked virgin. Satisfied that the back way was ruled out, he returned to the house.

In the hall he was joined by his sergeant, a man named Harry Dawson, who had been interviewing the neighbors. Dawson was a huge man and a great comfort to have around when things got tough—as well as an excellent companion at all times. He had a cheerful nature and a special dry humor of his own that could enliven the most sordid case. He also happened to be a good detective—observant, logical, and with an independence of view that made him invaluable to Grant as a mental sparring partner when a problem had to be thrashed out. Dawson, for his part, felt both respect and affection for Grant. He looked on him rather as the old maestro—more experienced than himself, broader in his knowledge and vision, a little more subtle—and with an endearing quality of slightly sonorous exposition which Dawson put down to the fact that he came from a line of schoolmasters. The two men had worked together on many cases and they made a formidable team.

"Well," Grant asked, "did anyone hear anything?"

"Not a thing, sir. They had the television on, both sides. *And* across the road . . . Worse than being asleep." Dawson grinned. "They're all pretty wide awake now, though."

"I'll bet they are!" Actually, Grant hadn't much hope of getting any direct evidence from the locals. The houses were too widely separated for indoor sounds to be easily audible to a neighbor. A car pulling up might have been different—but the murderer would hardly have risked drawing attention to himself by driving to the gate. He'd have parked somewhere and walked the last bit—and in this thinly populated suburb, shrouded in its trees, a man on foot could easily have approached the house and killed and slipped away again, unheard by anyone, unnoticed. Especially on a dark November night . . .

Grant told the sergeant about the lack of footmarks outside. "And there aren't any inside, either. Nothing on the parquet . . . The fellow must have wiped his shoes very thoroughly."

Dawson looked down at the mat by the front door. "Maybe the lab should have this, sir. . . . They might make something of it."

Grant nodded. "See to it, will you, Sergeant." He went back into the studio to complete his inspection there. For a moment or two he stood still, letting his gaze travel slowly around it as though he wanted to fix all the details in his mind before the pattern changed. His glance fell on the photograph frame and he stooped to look at the photograph. It was of a middle-aged woman with a narrow horse face, a tremendous nose, and close-set eyes under heavy brows. One of the ugliest female faces, Grant thought, that he'd ever seen anywhere. He moved down the long room, noting that none of the old furniture showed any sign of damage or disarray, that no drawers appeared to have been ransacked. He stopped for a moment before the cabinet, admiring its workmanship and thinking that it would look even better if it were properly dusted. He frowned over the fragment of glass on the desk—drawing no conclusions, but mentally recording a point for further consideration. He had a mind like a battery, storing impressions against the moment of need. He took a quick look at the pictures on the walls. Most of those with Lumsden's signature on them were of war scenes in Europe. One, a large and striking canvas, was a macabre painting in oil of scores of half-naked, near-skeleton bodies lying in grotesque attitudes. It was called "Belsen, 1945." Grant's slender nostrils widened in distaste. He wasn't qualified to judge it as a work of art, but he knew he wouldn't have fancied it on *his* wall. . . .

He turned as Dawson came in. "Right," he said, "let's see if the housekeeper's in better shape now."

He led the way across the hall into another sitting room. Kathie Bowen was hunched on a settee, sipping a cup of tea that a young policewoman had just handed to her. The rouge on her cheeks showed up as hectic spots against the whiteness of her face. Her eyes had a dazed, frightened look. Grant, in this moment of her disadvantage, put her age at forty-five—but he could see that she was a shapely and still attractive woman.

He drew up a chair beside her and sat down. "Are you feeling a bit better now, Mrs. Bowen?" he asked. His manner was gentle.

"A bit," she said. Her voice had just a trace of Irish breathiness.

"Has the doctor given you something?"

Kathie nodded.

"I'm afraid I'll have to ask you a few more questions," Grant said. "I'll try to keep them short. . . ."

Kathie nodded again. All the vitality had drained from her.

"What time was it when you left Mr. Lumsden, to go to your sister's?"

"Seven o'clock," she said.

"Exactly seven?"

"It might have been five past. It wasn't more. . . ."

"You happened to notice, did you?"

"Yes . . . I always went at the same time."

"Always . . . ? You mean you visited your sister regularly?"

"Yes, every Sunday."

"I see. . . . Could you give me her name, Mrs. Bowen, and tell me where she lives?"

"Eileen Marchant . . . She lives at one thirty-three, Elmore Road, Hendon."

The sergeant, standing by, made a note in his book.

"Good," Grant said. "And what time did you get back here?"

"Just after half past nine."

"Was that your usual time for getting back, too?"

"More or less."

"You had quite a routine," Grant said.

Kathie nodded. "It was John—he liked it that way. . . ."

"John?"

"Mr. Lumsden . . ."

"Ah—yes . . ." There was a slight pause. "And when you got back," Grant went on, "did you find everything just as *we* found it—apart from the telephone?"

Kathie's empty cup rattled in its saucer, and the policewoman took it away from her. "Yes," she said in a faint voice.

"You didn't touch anything else—the photograph frame, the glass, the chair . . . ?"

"No."

"You're quite sure about that?"

"Yes."

"Good . . . Now, about the telephone . . . You say it was turned over on its side, on the desk?"

"Yes . . . And the—the receiver—was hanging down over the edge."

"Could you hear anything?"

"There was a sort of—whirring noise."

"And what did you do?"

"I put the phone upright again, and joggled it, and after a bit the operator answered and I asked for the police."

"Can you remember which hand you held the receiver in?"

"The left, I think. . . . I usually do."

Grant nodded. Those fresh prints on the receiver, he thought, would almost certainly turn out to be Kathie's. "Well, that's all very clear," he said encouragingly. "Now—do you happen to know if Mr. Lumsden was expecting anyone to call on him this evening?"

"I'm sure he wasn't. He'd have told me."

"Have you any idea at all who might have wanted to kill him?"

Kathie shuddered. "No . . ."

"How long have you been Mr. Lumsden's housekeeper, Mrs. Bowen?"

"About a year."

"Was he a bachelor?"

"No—he was a widower."

"Ah . . . Did he have any children?"

"No."

"Do you know of any relative I could get hold of?"

"There's his nephew," Kathie said. "Michael. Michael Ransley."

"Where does he live?"

"In Barnet. Lancaster Mansions."

"That's not very far away, is it? Does he come here much?"

"He used to," Kathie said, "but he hasn't been lately."

"What about closer relatives? Didn't Mr. Lumsden have any brothers or sisters alive?"

"No . . . There's only Michael."

"I see. . . ." Grant looked down at his notebook. "Do you happen to know anyone with the telephone number Flaxman 0 0 six seven?"

"Yes," Kathie said. "That's George's. George Otway's."

"Who's he?"

"He's a friend of John's. . . ."

"Where does he live?"

"In Chelsea. Near Sloane Square . . ." Kathie's face crumpled. "George always comes here on Sunday evenings—but today he couldn't. . . . If he had, it wouldn't have happened. . . ." She gave a dry sob, and buried her head in her arms.

"There, there," Grant said, patting her shoulder. "You've been very brave—I won't bother you any more just now." He jerked his head meaningly to the policewoman, and got up. "We'll let your sister know what's happened, Mrs. Bowen—you'll be all right. I should try and get some rest. . . ." He went slowly out.

"Badly shocked, isn't she?" Dawson said.

Grant nodded. "It must have been a shocking thing for her—finding Lumsden like that. . . . Take a bit of getting over."

Back in the studio, he looked up Michael Ransley's number in the telephone book and dialed it. He got the ringing tone, but there was no reply. He hung up, and stood pondering.

"I think you'd better go round to Ransley's place and wait till he comes in, Sergeant. Tell him what's happened. Oh, and you'd better get his fingerprints. . . ."

"Right, sir."

"Drop them in at the Yard on your way home, will you. . . . I'll see you here in the morning."

"Very good, sir." Dawson put on his overcoat and went briskly out.

Grant picked up the phone again and dialed Flaxman 0067. Almost at once, a man's voice answered, giving the number.

"Mr. George Otway?" Grant asked.

"Speaking." The voice was firm and very pleasant.

"Good evening, sir—this is the police. Chief Inspector Grant. I'm afraid I've got some bad news for you."

"Oh, dear . . . What's happened?"

"It's Mr. John Lumsden, sir. He's been found dead."

"John . . . ? Oh, no!"

"That's not the worst of it, I'm afraid. . . ." Grant steeled himself—he always loathed this part of his job. "He's been murdered."

"Murdered . . . !"

"I'm very sorry, sir. I understand you were a friend of his. I'd like to come and have a talk with you if I may."

There was a moment of silence. Then the voice, no longer steady, said, "Of course . . . Come as soon as you like. . . . My God!"

4

In fact it was nearly half past eleven before Grant had completed his arrangements in Radlett and was able to get away. There was the removal of the body to supervise, the dispatch of a man to Eileen Marchant's, the provision of temporary care for Kathie. It took him another three quarters of an hour after that to drive himself to Chelsea through the thickening patches of mist. He found Otway's flat on the ground floor of a four-story Edwardian terrace, pleasantly situated at the end of a square. The curb was lined with residents' cars parked for the night and Grant had some difficulty in squeezing his own in. He spent a little time examining the three or four cars nearest the house before ringing the bell.

The man who came to the door was much younger than Grant had expected a friend of Lumsden's would be. He looked no more than thirty-five, and for a moment the inspector wondered if he'd

16

read the name plate wrongly. "Mr. Otway?" he asked doubtfully.

"That's right. . . ."

"Ah . . . I'm Chief Inspector Grant."

Otway nodded. "Please come in."

Under the hall light, Grant studied him for a moment. He was a big, dark, well-dressed, well-set-up man, almost as tall as Sergeant Dawson, with strong, clear-cut features. A man with a presence, Grant thought, and a very good-looking one—though now his face was set in the harsh lines of strain and shock.

"This way, Inspector," he said.

Grant preceded him into a spacious and attractive sitting room. Looking around, he saw that Otway shared John Lumsden's taste for expensive period furniture. Indeed, for good living generally . . . The curtains, the carpet, the sofa cushions, all looked as though they had been chosen without regard to cost. The color scheme was a delicate blend of ivory and gold. An ivory-colored telephone stood on a small table beside the sofa, flanked by two or three glossy magazines. Through an open door at the far end of the room Grant could see a gleaming mahogany desk, another telephone, bookshelves —the equipment of a study. On the floor by the door there was a suitcase with a hat and overcoat flung casually on top of it, as though someone had just come in from a journey or was about to start one.

Otway called, "Xanthe?" The name, as he spoke it, was like a chord struck softly on a harp.

A girl came out of the study, closing the door behind her.

"This is Inspector Grant," Otway said. "My wife . . ."

Grant said, "Good evening, Mrs. Otway," and the girl acknowledged him with a grave nod. She was a striking brunette of about thirty, tall and slim and very elegant, with a lovely oval face. . . . A remarkably handsome couple, Grant thought. . . . But now, like her husband, she looked tired and strained, and she sank at once onto the sofa, resting her head in her cupped hands.

Grant said, "I do apologize for troubling you at this late hour, Mrs. Otway—but I'm afraid it couldn't be avoided. . . . A dreadful business . . ."

"It's knocked us sideways," Otway said. "I can still hardly be-

lieve it. . . ." He waved Grant to a chair and took a seat opposite
him. "What happened, Inspector?"

"All I can tell you at the moment," Grant said, "is that someone
went to Mr. Lumsden's house tonight while Mrs. Bowen was out
and strangled him in his studio."

"*Strangled* him . . . Good grief!"

"There seems to have been a bit of a struggle. . . ."

"A struggle? With a man of his size and age!"

"How old was he, Mr. Otway?"

"About sixty-five."

"H'm . . . Well, it appears that he put up quite a fight, all the
same. A chair was overturned, things were broken, the phone was
hanging down. . . ."

At the mention of the phone, Otway gave a dejected nod. "I tried
to ring him this evening, but I couldn't get through—and the telephone people told us then that the receiver was off. It never occurred to us that there was anything wrong—we thought he'd just
forgotten to put it back. . . ."

"Of course," Grant said.

"Anyway, it must have been all over by then—we couldn't have
done anything. . . ."

"Not a thing, darling," Xanthe said. "You mustn't worry about
that. . . ."

Otway still looked very troubled. After a moment, he said, "Has
anyone managed to tell Mike Ransley—John's nephew? Someone
ought to. . . . I tried to ring him myself after you called, but he
was out."

"I've sent a man round to his house," Grant said.

"Ah, good. I wasn't much looking forward to breaking the news."
Slowly, incredulously, Otway shook his head. "What was the chap
after—money?"

"Apparently not . . ." Grant told them about the notecase. "As
far as we can tell at the moment, theft wasn't the object. We've
been all over the house, and nothing seems to have been disturbed."

"Did he break in?"

"No—the doors and windows are all intact. It looks as though
Mr. Lumsden let the man in himself."

"You mean it was someone he knew?"

"Well, we can't be certain of that—he *might* have asked a stranger in. But I wouldn't think so. It seems much more likely that he knew him."

Otway looked more bewildered than ever.

Xanthe said, "Who found him? Kathie, I suppose?"

"The housekeeper—yes."

"How awful for her . . . George, don't you think we ought to go over?"

"I wouldn't go tonight, Mrs. Otway. She's been given a sleeping pill—and there's a policewoman who'll keep an eye on her till morning."

Xanthe gave a little sigh of relief. "Oh—that's all right, then." She reached for a cigarette. Grant lit it for her. She had long, slim fingers, on one of which a big solitaire diamond flashed.

"The hell of it all is," Otway said, deep in his own thoughts, "that this would never have happened if I hadn't changed my plans. I usually visit John on Sunday evenings."

Grant nodded. "So Mrs. Bowen told me."

"We had a standing arrangement to play chess. Kathie always goes to her sister's on Sundays, and Xanthe likes to look at Sunday Night Theatre, so it fitted in well. . . ."

"How long have you had this arrangement with Mr. Lumsden?"

"About three months . . . I suggested a game one night when I was there, and John got so keen it became a regular thing. . . ."

"What time did you usually get there?"

"Oh—between a quarter and half past seven . . . We'd have a couple of drinks and a cold meal together, and then play till Kathie got back."

"What prevented you going tonight?"

"A sale up in Edinburgh I was interested in. I deal in pictures— keep an art shop in the King's Road. I expected to be catching the Night Scot, and I'd things to do, so I rang John this afternoon and told him I wouldn't be able to make it. The one night when it really mattered . . . !"

Grant glanced across at the suitcase on the floor. "So that's why you're all packed up?"

"That's it. . . ."

"You had a sleeper booked?"

"Sleeper—ticket—everything . . . If you hadn't rung me when you did, I'd have been on the train by now."

"But in fact you've been at home all the evening, have you?"

Otway gave the inspector a slightly startled look.

"It's just a routine question, Mr. Otway," Grant said. "We have to ask these things, you know."

"Of course . . . Yes, all the evening except for a short while around nine. I found I'd left the sale catalogue at the shop, so I drove round to get it. . . ." He produced the slim brochure from his pocket and briefly showed it to Grant. "The shop's only a few minutes away."

"What car do you drive?"

"A Ford Zodiac."

"The dark gray one standing outside the house now?"

"That's right."

Grant nodded. "That's why the engine was slightly warm."

Otway stared at him. "Heavens, you don't miss much."

"I try not to," Grant said, without complacency. He appeared to relax a little. "Well, now—I very much hope, Mr. Otway, that you may be able to give me some lead over this tragedy—that's really why I came to see you. . . . You evidently knew Mr. Lumsden pretty well."

"I knew him very well," Otway said. "We were the closest of friends."

"The age gap was wide. . . ."

"Yes, but that was part of it. John looked on me as a sort of protégé—and he was certainly a wonderful patron to me. . . . I owe him everything—don't I, darling?"

"We both do," Xanthe said.

"How did you come to know him?" Grant asked.

"It was one of those chance things—we happened to be visiting the Wallace Collection at the same time. I must have been about twenty-five. We were both looking at a battle picture, and we exchanged a few remarks about it, and then he started talking about modern war, said he'd been in the last one, asked me where I'd done my National Service. We walked round together for a bit and afterward we had a drink in a pub. . . . I told him I was very keen on pictures, though I couldn't paint myself. He told me he was an artist, and asked me if I'd like to see some of his work. I said I would, and he invited me to have lunch at his house next day—and that was how it all began. . . . He'd just lost his wife, and was rather lonely, not having any family of his own—and he seemed to take to me. When my father died soon afterward he virtually moved into the old man's place. He encouraged me to study, paid for me to travel and visit the famous galleries—and in the end he set me up in business. He bought me the lease of the art shop, stocked it, sent his friends along to it. He was marvelous. . . ." Otway broke off. "But I don't suppose you really want to hear all this, Inspector?"

"On the contrary," Grant said, "I'm most interested. . . . I need to know everything about John Lumsden—and at present I know practically nothing. Please go on. . . . What sort of man was he?"

For a moment, Otway didn't answer. His face showed deep distress. "It seems unbelievable—talking about him in the past tense." Then he pulled himself together. "Well—he was extraordinarily generous, as you'll have gathered. A very warmhearted man . . . Cultured, sensitive . . . He had a lively mind—lots of ideas—nice sense of humor. He was wonderful company. . . . I'll miss him terribly."

"H'm—I'd call that a panegyric rather than a character sketch," Grant said. "I can well understand how you feel about him—but couldn't you try to give me a more balanced picture? What about the other side of the slate? Had he no weaknesses?"

"I don't think he had any weaknesses in the sense you mean, Inspector. He didn't drink heavily—he wasn't a queer—there was nothing like that. . . ."

"I'll put it differently," Grant said. "Had he any peculiarities of personality?"

"Well, we all have those, don't we? He was inclined to act on impulse—but that's hardly a fault. He was unconventional—a bit eccentric, some people might say. He was temperamental, of course. He tended to worry about his health rather too much. He was prejudiced about a few things—but who isn't . . . ? He had a small bee in his bonnet about punctuality—couldn't bear things not to go according to schedule. Rather unusual in an artist . . . He was a bit of a *poseur* sometimes. . . . You asked me, so I'm telling you —but none of these things ever bothered me. He was a complex character—but a very likable one."

"Did he have a lot of friends?"

"About the usual number, I'd say. . . . Not as many, perhaps, as he sometimes made out—you could call that a weakness—but he certainly had dozens of acquaintances—too many, when he was painting. Kathie had to choke them off."

"Was he a good painter?"

Otway hesitated. "He had a fair talent—I wouldn't put it higher than that. Some painters are long on technique and short on feeling. John was the other way round. He had a great deal to say, but it didn't always come out in his work."

"Was he successful—commercially?"

"Not very . . . He's been selling a bit better in the last year or so but it took him a long while to get started. He wouldn't ever have been a really popular painter. For one thing, he didn't choose popular subjects."

"He seems to have been quite a well-to-do man," Grant said. "Presumably he had private means?"

"Oh, yes, his wife left him some money. That's how he was able to do so much for me."

Grant gave a thoughtful nod. "And what did he think of his work himself?"

"Oh, he was up and down about it. He got very depressed some-times—then I had to bolster him up. Other times he thought he was rather good—better than he was. . . . He was really rather unsure of himself—not just over his work, but everything. I think perhaps he had a slight inferiority complex."

"H'm . . ." Grant was silent for a moment. "As you describe him, he hardly sounds the sort of man to have made enemies."

"I wouldn't have thought so," Otway said. "Mind you, he could be quite outspoken, even belligerent—compensating for the unsure side of himself, I suppose—but there wasn't a scrap of malice in him. When you got to know him, you realized how essentially kind he was. I certainly never heard of any serious quarrel with anyone—and I think I would have done."

"You said he served in the war. . . . Did he talk much about those days?"

"Quite a bit. The war was the big experience in his life—there's no doubt it made a tremendous impression on him. . . . You've probably seen that Belsen canvas hanging in his studio."

"I have."

"Pretty grim, and not terribly good . . . I think he was trying to paint it out of his system."

"What did he do in the war?" Grant asked.

"He was something in Army Intelligence—went in after the battles and sorted things out. I don't think he did any fighting himself. From little phrases he dropped, I sometimes wondered if that worried him—the fact that he hadn't been in much personal danger. . . . He was a very conscientious man."

Grant said, "Intelligence is a field where a man might make enemies, I should think."

"Well, I doubt if he did. He wasn't involved in any cloak-and-dagger stuff, as far as I know—and he certainly never struck me as a man with dark secrets. He had anxieties—but they were mostly to do with his work."

"Any troubles over women?"

"I wouldn't think he had much to do with women after his wife died. He had an eye for them, the pretty ones, but he was shy of them and I'm sure he only admired from a distance. He was a bit handicapped, wasn't he, with his small size and—well—general appearance. . . . Not the sort of man a woman would go for at first sight."

"No, I suppose not. . . ." Grant appeared to have come to the end of his questions. Then he said, "By the way, what made him live at Radlett? Any special reason?"

"Only that he liked being north of London. He had a weekend cottage near Aldeburgh in Suffolk, and it meant he could reach it without having to drive through thick traffic."

"Did he go often?"

"He usually spent quite a bit of time there in the summer, if the weather was good. . . . He painted some of his most salable pictures up there, actually."

"Did he have friends in Suffolk?"

"I don't think so. He really went for seclusion."

A grandfather clock struck the hour of one. Grant looked at his watch—and then, apologetically, at Xanthe. "I've kept you late." He got to his feet. "So it boils down to this, Mr. Otway—you knew John Lumsden probably better than anyone, but you can't think of any reason why anyone should have wanted to kill him."

"It's completely beyond me," Otway said.

"Well—at least what you've told me has been very illuminating —and I dare say we'll turn something up. . . . What are your plans, by the way—will you be going to Edinburgh tomorrow?"

"No—I shan't go now."

"Then I'll let you know if there are any developments."

"I'd be glad if you would."

"Oh—there is one more thing before I leave. . . ." Grant picked up a small bag he'd brought with him, and opened it. "We've found various fingerprints in the studio, and there's just a chance the murderer's might be among them. To find out, though, we've first got to eliminate those that belong to the people who lived in the house, or visited it. Mr. Lumsden's own, of course, and Mrs. Bowen's —and I'll be getting Mr. Ransley's. Would you mind if I had yours? And your wife's, too, if she's been there lately. . . ."

"Of course," Otway said. "Anything to help . . ."

5

Grant snatched a few hours' sleep at his home in Putney and then drove quickly back to Radlett against the stream of the first commuters. When he was working on an interesting case he grudged any time spent away from it—and he had a growing feeling that this one *was* going to be interesting. The thing that intrigued him most at the moment was the fact that the murder had happened when it did. On any weekday night, Lumsden might have been out somewhere, or the housekeeper might have been at home with him. But Sundays normally had a rigid pattern. Grant had been much struck by the way the word "always" had constantly cropped up in the statements he'd so far been given. Sunday was the night Lumsden always stayed in to receive Otway. Sunday was the night Kathie always visited her sister—and she always left about seven and returned about nine thirty. Such regularity of behavior would have

25

been a gift to any prospective murderer—provided he'd known
about it. Even more intriguing was the *break* in the regularity on
the night of the murder. On any other Sunday Otway would have
been there, and able to prevent the crime. Had the murderer known
about that, too? Of course, it was just possible that someone with
a motive had called at Lumsden's without preknowledge, and
gained admittance, and killed because he'd happened to find the
circumstances favorable. But it seemed far more likely that the
killer had had inside information, and had gone there with intention. . . .

Grant was still thinking about it as he turned into Wilton Crescent.
Then, as he reached the drive, his interest switched. The time was
only a few minutes after eight, but it seemed that he wasn't the first
arrival at the house. A blue Morris Minor, which he hadn't seen
before, was parked in front of the garage. He thought at first that
it might belong to a reporter, but when he walked round it he saw
the name NORTH WESTERN WATER BOARD on the side, and a wad
of official papers on the back seat. Puzzled, he strode quickly to the
front door. He was even more puzzled when, glancing through the
sitting room window, he spotted the tops of two heads—a man's and
a woman's.

A young constable was on duty at the door. Grant said sharply,
"Who've you got in there?" jerking his head toward the sitting
room.

"Mr. and Mrs. Marchant, sir—the housekeeper's sister and
brother-in-law . . . They're waiting to take her home with them."

"Oh, I see. . . ." Grant relaxed. "Good . . . Where is Mrs.
Bowen?"

"Upstairs, sir, getting ready. Policewoman Evans is helping her.
. . . She won't be long."

"What sort of night did she have?"

"Very quiet, sir—gave no trouble at all."

"Has she had breakfast?"

"Just a cup of coffee, sir. She didn't want anything else."

Grant nodded, and went through into the sitting room. "Good
morning," he said briskly. "I'm Chief Inspector Grant."

"And I'm Eileen Marchant," the woman said.

Grant, studying her, could see little resemblance to Kathie. She was a short, very plump, blonde woman of about forty, with a figure that had obviously been left entirely to its own devices. Her hair looked as though it hadn't been touched that morning, and her vivid lipstick overlapped her mouth. Compared with the well-groomed Kathie, she was almost sleazy. But her eyes were the same —green and lively under attractively long lashes.

"This is my husband, Frank," Eileen Marchant said.

Marchant gave a barely perceptible nod. He was a tall, angular man, with a thin, bony face as unexpressive as a concrete post. If he had thoughts, they didn't show.

Grant turned back to Eileen. "So you're taking your sister home with you, Mrs. Marchant?"

"Indeed we are," Eileen said. "Where else would the poor soul go to at a time like this? Och, it's a dreadful thing to have happened." Her strong brogue and the vigor of her speech gave an impression of energy that Grant had hardly expected from her appearance.

"How is Mrs. Bowen this morning?" he asked politely.

"Why, she's had every bit of stuffing knocked out of her, and that's the truth," Eileen said. "She's like a creature walking in her sleep. . . ."

"She's had a bad shock," Grant said. "Still, I expect she'll get over it in a day or two."

"Do you, now!" Eileen looked very indignant. "Well, I can tell you she'll do nothing of the sort. She's not the kind to forget the man she was going to marry before he's even buried."

Grant gazed at her in astonishment. "*Marry?*"

"Did you not know? She was going to marry Mr. Lumsden—she told us about it last night. It was all settled between them—it was to be in two weeks' time, at the registrar's."

Grant shook his head. "I certainly didn't know. . . . Well . . . ! No wonder she's so upset."

"Och, she's the unfortunate one when it comes to marriage—a real jinx she has on her. . . . Did she not lose her first husband just six weeks after the wedding, in bitter circumstances—and now she's deprived once more and may well be a widow for the rest of her time. . . . All her life she's spent looking after people, first here, then there, and nowhere for long, nowhere a real home—and now when she had the chance to settle down at last, this had to happen. It's a tragedy."

"Yes," Grant said. "I'm very sorry."

Eileen looked at the watch on her pudgy wrist. "For God's sake, she should be down by now. . . . Frank has to be at work by nine, he's with the Water Board, what they call a water engineer, though I can't think why they give it the name. He's driving us home before he goes on, which is the kind, Christian thing to do. . . ."

She broke off as a step sounded on the stair. A moment later Kathie came in, wearing her fur coat, followed by Policewoman Evans carrying a small suitcase. Kathie said, "Hullo," to Grant in a flat voice. Her face was ashen, her eyes heavy. Beside her ebullient sister, she seemed lifeless. Marchant uncoiled himself and picked up the case. Eileen took Kathie's arm. "Well, good-bye, Inspector," she said. "I hope to God you find the devil who brought all this misery upon us."

"I'll do my best," Grant said. "Good-bye, Mrs. Bowen." Kathie murmured something inaudible. Marchant said, " 'Bye." It was the first time he'd opened his mouth during the whole interview.

Rather thoughtfully, Grant watched the little party get into the car.

6

It was a relief to have Kathie out of the way. Grant had deep personal sympathy for people whose lives were shattered as a result of a violent death, but professionally they were just an embarrassment—unless, of course, he wanted to question them. And, though Eileen's news had given him food for thought, he had no further questions to ask Kathie at the moment. There were more pressing things to do. . . .

He stood for a moment, considering his agenda. . . . All Lumsden's papers had to be gone through. All correspondence and effects had to be examined for a possible lead. The name of Lumsden's solicitor had to be found, and financial arrangements investigated. The fingerprint and medical reports would have to be studied as soon as they came through. And there was Michael Ransley to be seen—though he could wait until after Dawson had reported. . . .

Grant went into the studio. A chalk outline on the parquet now marked the spot where Lumsden's body had been found, and another on the desk indicated roughly where the telephone had been dangling. Otherwise there were no longer any signs of the tragedy. All the bits of broken glass had been gathered up and sent off to the Yard with the photograph frame. The chair was back in its place in front of the desk. Grant drew it out and sat down. Several of the desk drawers were locked but he had Lumsden's bunch of keys and he soon found the one that opened them. He took out an armful of letters and papers, lit his pipe, and settled down to examine them. The perusal of a dead man's effects was always a laborious job, but occasionally it was a rewarding one. A man's whole life could sometimes be reconstructed from the things he left behind. . . .

He had scarcely begun when the sergeant arrived. Dawson looked cheerful and ready for work, as always, but he was a little heavy around the eyes.

"Have a late night, Sergeant?" Grant asked.

"Bit late, sir . . . Ransley didn't come in until after two."

"M'm—bad luck . . . Not that I did much better myself. . . . Where had he been?"

"With a girl friend, he said."

"What's he like?"

"On the small side, like his uncle, but much better looking. About thirty, I'd say. Very cultured voice—sounds as though he went to Oxford twice! Works in the Foreign Office."

"How did he take the news?"

"It shook him rigid, sir—he practically couldn't speak."

"Did he have any ideas about who might have done it?"

"He said he hadn't—though I don't think he was trying. . . . I think he just wanted me to leave."

"You got his prints, did you?"

"Yes, after a bit of trouble. He wasn't very cooperative—not about anything. . . ."

"Oh, wasn't he? Well, I'll go and see him myself this evening."

Dawson nodded. "Any developments your end, sir?"

"I don't know about developments—but some quite interesting

information . . ." Grant gave the sergeant the gist of his overnight talk with George Otway. He also told him about Kathie Bowen's broken marriage hopes and her departure with the voluble Eileen and the silent engineer.

Dawson was as intrigued over the marriage plans as Grant had been. "It must have been a frightful blow to her, sir. . . . Quite apart from her feelings, I reckon she was onto a good thing. Well-heeled chap . . ."

"Yes," Grant said.

"Anyway, she's one person who wouldn't have wanted him dead."

"I shouldn't think so. . . ." Grant was always cautious about committing himself. He could look infinitely skeptical when he was examining a suspect, he could put forward the most damning hypotheses, but he preferred the clumsiest circumlocution to a premature accusation. "Never shoots till he sees the whites of their eyes," a colleague at the Yard had said of him. And, broadly, it was true.

"Well, pull up a chair," he said. "Let's get started on some of this stuff."

Dawson joined him at the desk and they settled to work. The sergeant concentrated on a file of recent correspondence. Grant sifted through a bunch of miscellaneous receipts, looked at some old check stubs going back several years, and carefully examined the dead man's passport. Lumsden, it seemed, had been quite a traveler—the record showed trips to Europe almost every summer, and several winter journeys to the Canaries, to Morocco, and to Egypt. From the passport Grant turned his attention to a bunch of old pocket diaries hoarded since 1950. Occasionally, one of the men would raise some point of interest, but mostly they worked in silence, making notes and setting aside anything that might conceivably prove useful later. They had done this job often together and knew exactly what they were looking for.

There was only one interruption. Around ten o'clock the telephone rang. It was Xanthe Otway, wanting to know if Kathie was still there and how she was getting on. Grant told her she'd left with her sister, and Xanthe said she'd call at the Marchants' that afternoon and take some flowers.

"Lady Bountiful," Grant murmured as he hung up. "Or something."

"What's she like?" Dawson asked.

"Lovely—but tall, bit on the thin side, rather aloof."

"Not your type, sir?"

Grant shook his head. "I like 'em short and sweet."

He pulled out another drawer. So far he had not come across any legal documents—but now, with an "Ah!" of satisfaction, he spotted one. It was a long, folded, double sheet of thick paper, with a bit of green ribbon running down the spine. "The last will and testament of John Edward Lumsden . . ." He was surprised that the will should be there, and not at a lawyer's or a bank, until he saw that it was only a draft. There were some penciled notes in one of the margins, and it wasn't signed.

Dawson had stopped work. "Anything interesting, sir?"

Grant read the draft through. "Well, according to this," he said, "Lumsden's estate is to be divided equally between Michael Ransley and George Otway. The nephew and the protégé . . . Fair enough, I suppose."

Dawson nodded. "I wonder how big the estate is."

"That's the next thing to find out," Grant said. He reached for the telephone book and looked up the number of the firm of solicitors named on the draft will.

7

An hour later, Grant was being shown into the office of the senior partner of Brett, Brett, Halliday and Brett, in Cannon Street. The partner's name was Forbes. He was a man of about sixty, with silky white hair and a brown, wrinkled face. He gave Grant an appraising look, and offered him a chair.

"I'm sorry you had to make the journey into town, Inspector—it's quite a trip from Radlett. . . . But I don't much care to discuss these confidential matters on the telephone."

"I quite understand, sir," Grant said. "It's perfectly all right. . . ."

"An appalling thing about Lumsden . . . I could hardly believe my eyes when I read the paragraph in the *Times* this morning. Truly appalling."

"Yes, indeed," Grant said.

33

"Such a brutal attack—and apparently so pointless. I gather that nothing was stolen. . . ."

"Not as far as we can tell," Grant said.

"Have you any clue to the assailant?"

"Not so far, I'm afraid." One of the troubles with his job, Grant reflected, was that other people always wanted to ask *him* questions. Understandable, of course—but time-wasting. Still, it usually paid to let them have their say and hold his own fire. Particularly with solicitors . . .

Unhurriedly, he opened his briefcase. "Did you know Lumsden well, sir?"

"I've known him a very long time. . . ." From Forbes's detached tone, it was clear that he felt no great sense of personal loss.

Grant nodded. "Well, this is the document I was talking about. . . ." He passed the draft will across the desk.

The solicitor put on his glasses and ran his eye down it. "Yes," he said, "this is very similar to the final version. . . . The only change of any consequence was a modest legacy to the Artists' Benevolent Fund—the other additions were quite minor. . . . The two young men still virtually share the estate."

"I'm told," Grant said, "that Michael Ransley is the only close relative. Is that right?"

"Yes, that is so. The family hasn't been at all fruitful in recent years, and there have been a lot of deaths. Ransley's parents were both killed in a car crash some years ago. His mother was Lumsden's sister."

"And George Otway, I gather, was regarded by Lumsden more or less as an adopted son?"

"That's right . . . I thought myself it was a very reasonable will in the circumstances—it took account of the blood relationship and gave expression to Lumsden's warm feelings for Otway at the same time. . . . I don't know either of the legatees well, but I've met them, and they both struck me as good types in their way. Ransley's an able and intelligent fellow, and Otway's very likable. . . . It's always pleasant when legatees appear deserving—so many aren't!"

Grant smiled. "When was the will made, sir?"

Forbes got up and went over to a filing cabinet "Ah—here we are. . . . Almost exactly two years ago . . . It replaced—rather belatedly—an earlier one in favor of his wife, who died."

"I see. . . . And would you mind telling me roughly, sir, the size of the estate?"

"Very roughly," Forbes said, "I should think it would be about two hundred thousand pounds, after death duties."

Grant gave him a startled look. "Two hundred thousand!"

"Something of that order. He inherited it all from his wife. She came of a wealthy publishing family."

"H'm . . ." Grant sat in silence for a moment or two. Then he said, "There was a photograph of a woman in Lumsden's studio—middle-aged, large nose, heavy eyebrows. . . . Was that his wife?"

"Yes—that was Edith Lumsden."

"Did you know her?"

"I met her several times."

"What was she like?"

"A battle-ax," Forbes said. "Very dominating."

"M'm . . . What do you suppose she saw in Lumsden? Talent?"

The solicitor gave a dry smile. "I think she just saw a husband, Inspector. . . . A woman with her sort of money wouldn't normally have had any difficulty in finding one, but she was excessively handicapped. You've seen her photograph. . . . I believe she'd been jilted, almost at the altar, not long before. And she wasn't young. Naturally I wouldn't say these things if the people concerned weren't both dead—but I fancy she married Lumsden as a desperate last resort."

"What about him? Presumably he *did* marry her for her money?"

"In a way, I suppose he did—though I think all he really wanted at that time was freedom to paint. He was an art teacher at some polytechnic when he met Edith—pretty exhausting work, and not much pay. Marriage to her offered leisure, travel, stimulus—it must have seemed an irresistibly tempting opportunity. . . . Anyhow, he was probably swept along. Edith was a very powerful personality."

"How did the marriage work out?"

"Oddly enough, not too badly—on the surface, at any rate. She took good care of Lumsden, mothered him, encouraged him in his work. . . . And he relied on her. Not a very romantic union, I'd think—but perhaps not entirely a failure. . . ."

"H'm . . ." Grant shook his head. "It doesn't sound very exciting to me. . . ."

8

Instead of returning to Radlett from the solicitor's, as he'd intended, Grant drove straight to his office at the Yard. For the moment he was no longer interested in Lumsden's papers—his thoughts were concerned exclusively with Forbes's disclosure about the size of the estate. Two hundred thousand pounds! Now that was a prize worth gambling for in a really big way—a glittering fortune, even if it had to be shared. With that amount of money accruing from Lumsden's death—and liable to be lost if he hadn't died—the financial motive was clearly the one to look into first. Otway and Ransley might both be "good types," as Forbes had said—but they might not. Both of them would certainly have been well equipped, Grant thought, to do the sort of "inside" job that the facts pointed to. Otway and Ransley . . . Well, he'd seen Otway. Now he'd take a look at Ransley. . . .

There were a couple of reports waiting for him on his desk, and he paused for a moment to glance through them. One related to the mat that Dawson had removed from Lumsden's hall. The analyzed scrapings had revealed nothing of special interest—nothing that might not have been brought in by any caller. The other was the medical report—which told Grant little more than he knew already. The indicated time of death was well within the limits set by the other evidence. Only moderate force, it seemed, had been required from the strangler on Lumsden's stringy neck—which meant that any man of average strength could have committed the crime. Bruises, incurred before death, had been found on Lumsden's left thigh and upper right arm, but they had not been severe and he appeared to have suffered no other injuries except the fatal one. It looked, therefore, as though the struggle had been slight. Possibly, Grant thought, it had amounted to no more than clumsy evasive action by Lumsden. That would have been enough to account both for the bruises and for the upset in the studio. . . .

He put the medical report down and picked up the phone. "I want to speak to Mr. Michael Ransley at the Foreign Office," he told the switchboard. "Ring me back, will you?"

He had barely replaced the receiver when a colleague looked in— a man named Jarvis from the fingerprint department. He had a file under his arm. "Hullo, Charlie," he said affably. "I hoped you'd be in. It's this Radlett case."

"Got something for me?" Grant asked.

"I'll say—it should gladden your heart. . . . Take a look at this." Jarvis produced a sheet of paper and some photographs and proudly presented them.

Grant read through the brief typed report. Then, fascinated, he studied the photographs. *"Well!"* he exclaimed.

"Solved your case, haven't we?"

"M'm—it does rather look like it. . . . Did you find anything else?"

Jarvis snorted. "What else do you need, for Pete's sake?"

The telephone rang. Grant stretched for the receiver. It was the switchboard. "About your call to the Foreign Office, sir. They say Mr. Ransley's in conference and want to know if it's urgent."

"Forget it," Grant said. "Get me Sergeant Dawson at Radlett eight two, will you? I'll hang on."

"Well, good luck with the arrest," Jarvis said. "I'll leave the dabs with you." He went out.

In a moment Dawson came on the line. "Hullo, sir . . ."

Grant said, "I'd like you to get down to the office right away, Sergeant. We're going to pay a call on Mr. Otway."

9

Dawson got to the Yard just at lunchtime and Grant put him in the picture over a chop in the canteen. For an hour they discussed the significance of the new development and the best tactics to employ. First, Grant thought, they should do a bit more probing into Otway's background while he was still unsuspicious. After that, a stiff interrogation—and action would depend on what he had to say. . . . Dawson agreed.

At two thirty they left in a police car for the Chelsea art shop. They found it on the north side of the King's Road, not far from the Town Hall. Its exterior was modest, even a bit drab, but the shop itself had a flourishing air. There were five or six customers standing around, several in attitudes of slight impatience. Two men and a girl were serving. There was no sign of the owner. Grant went up to the girl. "Is Mr. Otway about?" he asked quietly.

"Yes, sir, he's inside. . . ."

"Then please go and tell him Chief Inspector Grant would like to see him."

The girl finished tying a parcel, gave it to a customer, and went off. Grant and Dawson took the opportunity to look around the shop. It was a long, narrow room, stacked with artists' equipment of every kind. There were rolls of canvas, shelves of paint, palettes and easels and brushes, sheets of glass, and frames of every size and quality. Pictures with price labels were on display in the window and on the walls. One of them, Grant noticed, was by John Lumsden. It was priced at fifteen guineas.

The girl returned. "Will you come this way, please?" The two men followed her into an inner room, comfortably furnished as a private office. Otway was sitting behind a desk. He got up as the policemen entered. "Hullo, Inspector . . ." He had the subdued air of a man still not quite recovered from a bad shock.

"This is Sergeant Dawson," Grant said.

Otway nodded to the sergeant.

"There are some things I have to discuss with you, Mr. Otway. . . . It may take a little time."

"I see. . . ." Otway's manner showed interest, but not the least trace of perturbation. "All right, make yourselves comfortable." He found them chairs. "I won't keep you a moment. . . ." He lifted the receiver of an intercom set on his desk and pressed a button. There was a loud buzz in the room outside, which went on for some time. It would have been quicker, Grant thought, if Otway had stepped into the shop himself instead of behaving like a tycoon. Absurd, in such a small place . . . But at last someone answered.

"Oh, Peter," Otway said, "will you look after Mr. Finch when he calls—I'm going to be busy for a while and I don't want to be disturbed. . . . That's right—three o'clock. Something about a new line in synthetic canvas . . . Thanks."

He hung up, and looked across at Grant. "Well, Inspector, what's on your mind? Have you got anywhere with the case?"

"I think we've made a little progress," Grant said.

"You have? Good . . ."

"Before we get on to that, though, I wonder if you could give me some more particulars about yourself. I'm building up a dossier on everyone who knew John Lumsden—just for the record. . . . You told me quite a bit last night—but there are still some gaps."

"Well, I'll be happy to fill them," Otway said. "What is it you want to know?"

"Oh, the usual biographical things. Place and date of birth, father's name and profession, family details, education . . ."

Otway nodded. "Well, I was born in Hammersmith on February twelfth, nineteen twenty-eight. My father was John Edward Otway. He worked in the Art Department of the *Daily Record* most of his life. He died in nineteen fifty-four, four years after my mother. I've no brothers or sisters. I was educated at Collett's School, Carshalton —public, very minor! No university—the old man couldn't run to it. . . ."

"What about National Service? I seem to remember you mentioned it."

"Yes—from forty-six to forty-eight. Pretty undistinguished—though I did manage to get a commission."

"And a good conduct discharge, I don't doubt."

Otway smiled. "Yes—they never rumbled me!"

"Then what?"

"Then I did various jobs—I couldn't seem to get settled. . . . I tried my hand at newspaper reporting, I worked in an estate agent's office for a bit, I even had a bash at selling motorcars."

"I see. . . . This was before you developed your interest in art, I take it?"

"Oh, not at all. I was always very interested—but as I told you I've no creative talent myself and I couldn't see a way of making a living out of it. What I always wanted to do was to combine art with business—which I have got some talent for—and as you know the lucky break came when I met John—in nineteen fifty-three. I opened the shop in nineteen fifty-five and I haven't looked back."

"When did you marry?"

"Two years ago . . . My second lucky break."

Grant nodded. "Well, that seems to take care of your career, Mr. Otway. . . . Now I wonder if you could give me similar details about your wife?"

Otway looked a bit surprised. "I can give you something. . . . Let me see. . . . Xanthe was born in nineteen thirty-six, in Pimlico. She was an only child, too. She went to school in London—just an ordinary L.C.C. school. Her father's name was Alfred—Alfred Hepple. . . ."

"What did he do?"

"Played the horses mostly, I think! But he had some sort of job as a commission agent."

"Is he alive?"

"Well—we don't really know. . . . He and Xanthe's mother were divorced and he cleared off to South America—hasn't been heard of since."

"Is your wife's mother still alive?"

"No—she died in nineteen fifty-three."

"Did she marry again?"

"She did, but I gather it didn't work out. . . ."

"It must all have been rather upsetting for a young girl," Grant said.

"Yes—Xanthe did have a bit of a rough passage."

"Being left alone at seventeen, too. . . . What did she do?"

"She settled in digs with a few other girls and got herself a job modeling clothes. She did quite well in the end, too—she was with Cleaver and Jones when we married. Hard work—but not badly paid."

"Does she still model?"

"No—now she just looks after me. Anything else, Inspector?"

"Thank you—I think that's about all. . . . You've given me a very good picture."

"Right . . . Now what about the case?"

Grant shifted his chair slightly, so that he had a better view of Otway's face. "Well, as I said there've been a few interesting developments. This morning we found a draft of John Lumsden's will in his desk."

"Oh, yes?"

"It seems that you and Michael Ransley are co-heirs to Lumsden's estate. Did you know?"

"Yes, I knew. John told us just after he made the will—a couple of years ago. He had us along for a little celebration—complete with toasts and speeches. I think he got quite a kick out of it."

"When we talked yesterday, Mr. Otway, you agreed that he was probably a well-to-do man. Have you any idea of the actual size of the estate?"

Otway shook his head. "Not even a rough one."

"H'm . . . I'd have thought he might have got a kick out of mentioning a figure, too."

"No . . ."

"Well," Grant said, "I'm told that the total after death duties could be two hundred thousand pounds."

Otway stared at him. "As much as that!"

"So I'm informed. A hundred thousand each—tax free. . . . Enough to keep you in luxury for the rest of your life. Quite a prospect for you, isn't it?"

Until now, Otway had seemed relaxed, if a little puzzled. Now he looked distinctly annoyed. "Well, it doesn't give me any pleasure at the moment, I can tell you."

"It will later, though, won't it?" Grant said. "Unless you're already such a wealthy man in your own right that you don't need it. Are you?"

"Of course not . . ."

"A business like this needs a lot of capital, I imagine."

"What business doesn't? I don't see . . ."

"And you have rather expensive personal tastes, Mr. Otway. You enjoy luxury. So, I've noticed, does your wife. . . ."

Otway's handsome face darkened. "You're being remarkably offensive, Inspector. . . . What the hell's all this got to do with the case?"

"I'm coming to that," Grant said. "Did you know that John Lumsden was planning to marry Mrs. Bowen?"

"I didn't *know*. Was he?"

"So her sister told me this morning. In a fortnight, she said."

"I hadn't heard that."

"Strange that Lumsden didn't tell you—such a close friend."

"He'd probably have told me last night. I suppose he'd just made up his mind."

"Anyhow, you're not surprised?"

"Not a bit—it was obviously on the cards. Mike Ransley's been prophesying it for ages. . . . Anyone could see they got on well together."

"If Lumsden had married Mrs. Bowen," Grant said, "he would probably have altered his will."

"Almost certainly, I should think."

"Mrs. Bowen might even have had a child by him. Then the whole of the estate might have stayed in the family. You might have got nothing."

"I don't think John would have gone that far," Otway said. "I might have got very little. . . ." He was gazing hard at Grant. "What exactly are you driving at, Inspector?"

"I'm suggesting, Mr. Otway, that from a purely financial point of view it might have been to your advantage to kill John Lumsden before he had time to remarry."

Otway's jaw dropped. He looked so utterly taken aback that at that moment Grant could have sworn the reaction was genuine. "Me kill John! You must be out of your mind."

"I'm merely putting it to you," Grant said, "that you would have had a strong motive."

"Well! I don't know what to say. . . . It's unbelievable."

"Don't you agree that you'd have had a motive?"

"I'd have had a motive, yes—but I wouldn't have done it in a million years. . . . So would Mike Ransley have had a motive, for that matter—though I'm damned sure he wouldn't have done it either. Why pick on me?"

"Because, Mr. Otway, we found some of your fingerprints in the studio."

"What's odd about that? They must be all over the place."

"These were in a rather special place."

"Oh? Where?"

"There was a small framed photograph in the studio. A photograph of Lumsden's late wife. You know it, of course."

"Naturally . . ."

"Apparently it was knocked off the desk during the struggle. The glass broke, and fell out of the frame in pieces. We found one of the pieces on top of the desk. It had your fingerprints on it."

"Why shouldn't it have? I was looking at that photograph only last week. It's always fascinated me. . . ."

"Did you take the photograph and the glass out of the frame when you looked at it?"

"Of course I didn't," Otway said impatiently.

"Have you ever done so?"

"No—why on earth should I? Why do you ask?"

For a moment, Grant didn't answer. Then in a slightly milder, more argumentative tone, he said, "Because, Mr. Otway, your prints were on *both* sides of the piece of glass. A thumbprint on one side, and two fingerprints close together on the other. . . . In view of what you've just said, the only possible conclusion seems to be that you held it in your hand after the glass was broken. Last night, in fact . . ."

"I certainly didn't."

"Then how do you account for the prints?"

"Someone must have made a mistake."

"There's no mistake about whose they are," Grant said, "I can tell you that. They're yours, all right."

"They *can't* be. . . ." Otway shook his head, as though trying to free himself from some entangling mental thicket. "Anyway, it doesn't make sense. Why would I pick up the glass—just one piece —and leave it on the desk? I'd have been crazy."

"Well, I've given some thought to that myself," Grant said, "and it seems to me there could be quite a simple explanation. Murderers don't always act sensibly. Or coolly. Especially amateur murderers . . . The shock of actually throttling a man to death would be pretty upsetting, don't you think? Particularly a man who'd struggled for his life, who'd sent chairs and telephones flying . . . The noise, the breaking glass . . . Most unnerving, I'd say. I can well imagine our murderer starting to pick up the glass mechanically—then realizing there was no point in trying to clear up the traces of the struggle —and, in his hurry to get away, overlooking the danger of the piece he'd already picked up. It's unplanned panic that hangs most killers."

"Maybe it is," Otway said. "I wouldn't know. . . . I still say it would have been crazy. And I can tell you this, Inspector—if I'd done it I'd have worn gloves. Then there wouldn't have been any prints."

"You could have worn gloves and still made this mistake," Grant said. "You could have taken them off for the strangling—to get a better grip. Then picked up the glass in a kind of daze. Then put the gloves on again. It's quite possible."

"It may be possible . . . All I can say is, it wasn't me."

"You had a motive," Grant said. "And now it seems that you were there."

"I was *not* there. I told you, I was at home all the evening."

"I've only your word for that. And a set of fingerprints that appear to prove you weren't."

"My wife was with me. She'll tell you."

"With respect," Grant said, "that wouldn't help at all. Did you have any visitors during the evening?"

"No—we were alone."

"That's a pity."

"Wait a minute, though. I tried to ring John just before eight— remember? From the house. That proves I was there."

Grant looked at him thoughtfully. "Ah, yes—the abortive call . . . By the way, what was it you wanted to talk to Lumsden about?"

"About one of the pictures in the sale."

"Without having the catalogue to refer to?"

"I didn't need it—the picture was one I knew about. I wanted his advice."

"How many times did you dial his number before you gave up?"

"I think we rang three times altogether, over about ten minutes. It didn't seem likely he'd be talking to anyone else for that long— he was usually rather brief on the phone. So then we asked the supervisor to check."

"*We*, Mr. Otway? According to the supervisor, it was a woman who spoke to her."

Otway's face fell. "Yes—that's right. . . . I called John in the first place, but it was my wife who asked for the number to be checked."

"How was that?"

"She happened to have the phone—she was ringing TIM to get the right time. I asked her to have another go at John, and she did, and when she still couldn't get through she called the supervisor."

"H'm . . . Well, we're no further forward then, are we? We still haven't any proof that you were at home."

"No . . ." Otway looked blankly at the inspector. Then, suddenly, his expression changed again. Relief came flooding in. "What a fool I am! *Of course*—I had a call from Whybrow. . . ."

"Who's Whybrow?"

"He's an employee of mine—my buying assistant. He rang me up from Edinburgh last night."

"When?"

"About half past seven."

"Really . . . What did *he* ring about?"

"About the sale . . . I'd sent him up to give the pictures the once-over. I usually do when the sale's a long way away—it saves me a journey in case the stuff turns out to be disappointing. I asked him to ring me and report—and he did. He said some of the pictures were worth bidding for. So I was going to get the Night Scot, as I told you."

"H'm . . . Most interesting . . . I'd like every detail of that call, Mr. Otway, from the beginning. Did *you* answer the phone when it rang?"

"No—my wife did."

"If you were expecting the call, why didn't you?"

"I was in the study—the next room."

"You spoke from the extension there?"

"It isn't an extension—it's a separate line. . . . My wife called to me, and I went into the sitting room."

"How long did you talk to Mr. Whybrow?"

"Oh—three or four minutes—I don't know exactly. . . . The phone people will be able to tell you."

Grant looked a bit nonplussed. "Well, it's all very strange."

"It's the truth, Inspector—you can check it for yourself. . . . And surely that lets me out. John must have been killed after Kathie left him—and she usually goes about seven. And the telephone receiver was off by ten minutes to eight. Isn't that right? Wasn't he killed between seven and eight?"

"Something like that," Grant said.

"There you are, then—I *am* in the clear. What's more, I think you owe me a very humble apology. This has been a pretty bad half hour for me, I can tell you."

"What about the fingerprints?"

"That's your worry, Inspector. Obviously there must be some explanation. Anyway, it's plain enough I couldn't have done it."

Grant looked at Dawson. They both got up.

"Well, we'll see," Grant said, in his most noncommittal tone.

10

They drove straight back to the Yard. Dawson had a thwarted look; he had been confidently expecting the interrogation to be followed by a routine caution and Otway's arrest. Fingerprints had never let him down before, and he couldn't believe they had done so now. Fingerprints, it was well known, were the most reliable evidence of all. . . . Grant was in a state of suspended judgment. He had been impressed by Otway's attitude—especially by one aspect of it—but there were a lot of things he wanted to know about that crucial telephone call. The moment he reached the office he set to work to check up on it—with a thoroughness that, one way or another, would leave the issue in no doubt.

First, he got in touch with the telephone authorities in Edinburgh. From them, after a brief delay, he learned that a call had in fact been made by a Mr. Whybrow to Flaxman 0067 on the previous evening. It had been a transferred charge call, which was why the caller's name was known. It had been made from the Northern Hotel, Edinburgh. Connection had been established at 7:32 P.M. and the call had lasted four minutes. The charge had been debited to Flaxman 0067 in the usual way.

Late in the afternoon, with more help from the telephone people, Grant managed to track down the operator who had actually rung the Flaxman number. Her name was Rose Foreman, and she sounded both alert and responsible.

Grant said: "I want you to think very carefully, Miss Foreman, before you reply to my questions, because a great deal may depend on what you say. . . . First of all, who answered at Flaxman 0 0 six seven when you rang the number last night? A man or a woman?"

"A woman," the operator said.

"What did you say to her?"

"I said, 'Is that Flaxman 0 0 six seven?' and she said it was. I said, 'I have a transferred charge call for you from a Mr. James Whybrow in Edinburgh. Will you accept it?' "

"What did she say?"

"Oh—something like 'Yes, put him through.' "

"Was that all you heard?"

"I heard her call out, 'George, it's Whybrow.' "

"Did you? You have a good memory, Miss Foreman."

"It was the unusual name—Whybrow. It sort of stuck in my mind."

"The line must have been very clear."

"It was."

"Well, then what happened?"

"Then I heard the caller speak to another man."

"Did you hear what they said to each other?"

"Oh, no—it was only for a second. I was just making sure the connection was satisfactory."

"I see. . . . Is there any possibility, would you think, that the second voice at the Flaxman end *wasn't* a man's voice?"

The girl seemed very surprised. "No—it was a man's, all right."

"Couldn't it have been a woman speaking very low, pretending to be a man?"

"Not unless she was a most *peculiar* woman," the girl said.

Grant smiled to himself. "Well, thank you very much, Miss Foreman. . . . You've been an excellent witness."

11

An hour later Grant rang the Northern Hotel and spoke to James Whybrow. The inspector was eager to see what sort of man he was, as well as to question him, and when he learned that Whybrow was planning to return to London that evening by the Night Scot he decided it would be better to postpone the examination and meet him when he got off the train. For purposes of recognition, he asked for a brief description. Whybrow, it seemed, would be hatless, wearing a fawn duffel coat, and carrying a brown Globetrotter suitcase. Grant named the platform barrier as the rendezvous and Whybrow said he'd keep a lookout.

Grant arrived at King's Cross station next morning well before the Edinburgh train, which was late—but when it drew in, the prearranged contact was made without any difficulty. Whybrow proved to be a tall, thin man, around fifty, with a lined, rather anxious face and nicotine-stained fingers. At Grant's suggestion they repaired to the lounge of the station hotel to have their talk over a pot of coffee.

"Is it something about Mr. Lumsden?" Whybrow asked, as they sat down.

"It's to do with him, yes."

"I thought it must be. What a dreadful thing to have happened. . . ."

"When did you hear about it?"

"It was in the *Scotsman* yesterday morning. And then Mr. Otway phoned me. . . . It's been a frightful blow to him. They were very close, you know."

"So I understand. . . ." Grant produced cigarettes as the coffee came, but Whybrow said he preferred to stick to his own brand. "Did you know John Lumsden, Mr. Whybrow?"

"I met him a couple of times at the shop—that's all."

"How long have you been with Mr. Otway?"

"About three years."

"What do you think of him?"

Whybrow looked a little taken aback at the direct question.

"Strictly off the record," Grant said.

"Well—he's not too bad. Lots of charm, when he likes to switch it on. Fancies himself a bit, maybe. Very shrewd and capable. You need to be, in this business."

"I suppose it's highly competitive?"

"Very . . . You can lose money as easily as make it."

"Has Mr. Otway a good eye for a picture?"

"He has a good eye for a picture that'll sell," Whybrow said. "A flair for the market . . . On artistic values, I must say I prefer my own judgment."

"That's very natural. . . . What did you do before you joined Mr. Otway?"

"Writing, mostly . . ."

"About pictures?"

"Yes . . . Articles, reviews—free-lance work." Whybrow gave a wintry smile. "Precarious sort of life—I was glad to have finished with it."

"I can imagine." Grant took a sip of coffee. "Are you married?"

"Yes."

"Children?"

"A boy and a girl. Fourteen and sixteen . . ."

"Just coming up to the expensive age," Grant said.

"Oh, they did that years ago. . . ."

"Quite a struggle, eh?"

"It is, rather."

Grant nodded—and paused. "Well, now, Mr. Whybrow, I'm going to ask you a few questions that I think may help me in this case. You'll probably think that some of them sound rather odd, but I don't want you to get any wrong ideas. They're just a routine check on information I've been given. Okay?"

"Sure," Whybrow said. "Fire away."

"First of all, then, about this trip of yours. I gather you went to Edinburgh for a preview of some pictures and that Mr. Otway was going to join you for the sale if your report was satisfactory. Is that right?"

"Quite right."

"I'm told that you often make such trips."

"Yes—probably a dozen times in a year."

"Was there anything at all unusual about this one?"

"Nothing at all."

"When did Mr. Otway give you your instructions about it?"

"He'd been talking about it for some days—but we had a final word on Saturday evening, at the shop."

"Saturday *evening?*"

"Well—early evening . . . I left him just after six."

"Does he usually work so late on Saturdays?"

"Not usually—but he had something he wanted to finish. . . ."

"I see. . . . And when did you travel up to Edinburgh?"

"On Saturday night."

"When was the preview?"

"All day Sunday. I went in the afternoon."

"And you telephoned Mr. Otway from the Northern Hotel on Sunday evening?"

"Yes."

"Where did you speak from? A public box?"

"No, the box was occupied. I spoke from the reception counter in the lobby."

"A transferred charge call, I'm told."

"Yes."

"Why did you transfer the charge?"

"I always do when I ring Mr. Otway from a distance," Whybrow said. "It saves bothering about change if the conversation runs on."

"But if you were speaking from the counter, you didn't need change. There wasn't a coin box, was there?"

Whybrow looked a bit surprised. "Well, no . . ."

"The call could have been charged on your bill."

"It could have been—I didn't think of it. . . . I'd got into the habit of transferring the charge, that's all."

"It's a good reason," Grant said. "Now what time did you make this call?"

"At half past seven."

"Exactly at half past seven?"

"Within a minute or two."

"How is it you're so sure?"

The corners of Whybrow's mouth turned down a little. "Mr. Otway asked me to ring him at seven thirty. . . . He's my boss!"

"A bit of a martinet, is he?"

"He likes to have his instructions carried out."

"And makes a fuss if they're not?"

"He does, rather. . . . I got a rocket a few weeks back for being fifteen minutes late with a call."

"Is that why you phoned from the counter instead of waiting for the public box to become free?"

"That's right. . . . Not that I'm complaining—I like a man to know his own mind."

"Did Mr. Otway say why he wanted you to ring at that particular time?"

"No—I suppose it just suited him. . . . Between drinks and dinner, you know! I usually ring about then, if it's on the week-end."

"I see. . . ." Grant paused. "Well, now, here's the first odd question. Are you quite sure it *was* Mr. Otway you spoke to?"

Whybrow stared at him. "But of course . . ."

"You recognized his voice?"

"Naturally."

"You've no doubt about it?"

"None whatever."

"Was the line good?"

"Well, it could have been better—but it was Mr. Otway all right. There's absolutely no question about that."

Grant nodded. "I just wanted to make sure. How did the conversation go—can you remember?"

"More or less . . . I said I'd been to the preview and that there were several pictures I thought Mr. Otway would be interested in, and I mentioned some of them, and he asked me a question or two, and then he said, right, he'd come up on the night train and we'd have breakfast together at the Northern in the morning and discuss plans. That was about all. . . ."

"H'm . . ." Grant sat back, studying Whybrow's face. The anxious look was still there—but it hadn't deepened. The man looked puzzled, that was all. Still . . .

"You say you made this call from the counter, Mr. Whybrow. Now I'm not doubting anything you've told me, not in the least— but whenever possible I like to check. Was there anyone else at the counter when you were talking?"

"Yes," Whybrow said, "the receptionist was there. A man . . ."

"Could he have heard what you were saying?"

"He could if he'd wanted to."

"What was he like?"

"A youngish man—about twenty-five—dark—black hair . . ."

Grant finished his coffee and got up. "Thank you, Mr. Whybrow. I'm much obliged to you. Can I give you a lift anywhere?"

12

From his desk at the Yard, half an hour later, Grant rang the Northern Hotel again and asked for the manager. "This is the Metropolitan Police," he said. "Chief Inspector Grant . . . I'd like to have a word with one of your receptionists—a man of about twenty-five, with black hair. . . . I don't know his name."

"That would be Fowler," the manager said. "He's not in any trouble, I hope?"

"None at all . . . I just want to check something with him."

"Well, hold on, will you?"

A minute passed, two minutes . . . Then another man came on the line. "Fowler here . . . Yes, Inspector?"

"I'm inquiring," Grant said, "about a telephone call that was made by one of your guests from the reception counter at seven thirty on Sunday evening. Were you on duty then?"

"I was, sir."

"Do you remember the call? It was made by a Mr. Whybrow—a tall, thin man, about fifty."

"Oh, yes, I remember. The box was busy and he was in a hurry to get through. . . . A transferred charge call to London, wasn't it?"

"That's the one. Now I'm very anxious, Mr. Fowler, to check the conversation that took place. Did you happen to catch any of it at all?"

"Well, let me think, sir. . . . Not much, I'm afraid. Something to do with a sale of pictures. Oh, yes, and the man he was talking to was going to join him here for breakfast. That's about all, sir."

"*Was* it a man he was talking to?"

"Yes, sir."

"How do you know?"

"Well, I could hear his voice through the receiver. . . ."

"Oh, you could. . . . You're quite sure of that?"

"Positive, sir."

"All right, Mr. Fowler, thank you very much. . . ." Grant hung up.

So that, he thought, was that. . . .

13

Now Grant's interest switched to transport problems and time schedules. . . .

It was, he reckoned, about eighteen miles from Chelsea to Lumsden's house at Radlett. Most of the route was built up, with pretty heavy traffic at all times, and dozens of traffic lights. Driving conditions on Sunday evening had been very bad. Grant himself had taken all of fifty minutes to reach the Otways' flat from Radlett. A driver ignoring speed limits and taking chances could still not have covered the distance in less than half an hour. More likely forty minutes . . .

Otway, assuming now that he'd talked on the telephone at his house at seven thirty, wouldn't have had more than twenty minutes for the trip whichever way he'd worked it. . . . If he'd gone to Radlett early and done the job immediately Mrs. Bowen had left the house, he couldn't have started for home before ten past seven, at the earliest. So that was out—he wouldn't have had a hope of getting home by seven thirty. If he'd waited till after the phone call, he'd have had to be in Radlett before ten minutes to eight. Again, only twenty minutes—less . . . It was out of the question.

That was always supposing, of course, that the time limits they'd accepted for the murder were reliable. Grant considered them again. Mrs. Bowen had been quite definite about when she'd left—and the inspector could see no reason why she shouldn't have told the truth. . . . And Lumsden would never have left the receiver hanging down like that, buzzing away, if he'd been alive. Besides, the limits tied in perfectly with the medical report, which had put the time of death at around seven thirty, give or take half an hour or so. And with other things—like the fact that Lumsden had just begun his evening meal. Taken together, the evidence on the time of death was overwhelming. . . . Clearly, those limits had to be accepted.

In which case, George Otway had a complete alibi. . . .

14

In a cynical and frustrated moment, Grant had once been heard to observe that the man to concentrate on in any criminal case was the one with the best alibi. It had been a passable crack, but that was all. . . . Grant knew very well that the alibis the guilty tried to rig up for themselves were rarely good ones—they were usually shoddy jobs, lash-ups that fell apart at the first test. Whereas innocent persons nearly always *did* have good alibis. Not many people spent much time absolutely alone, with no witnesses of their actions, of their comings and goings. They visited or they had visitors, they made telephone calls or received them, they stopped at garages for gas, they watched television with their children, they drank in pubs with their cronies, they nodded to the cinema manager on their way into the pictures. . . . There was usually someone to speak up for the innocent, to remember seeing them. And a good thing, too.

. . . It was alibis, more than anything, that made the elimination of innocent suspects possible and speedy. Alibis should be welcomed. . . .

Yet Otway's alibi left Grant with a strong feeling of dissatisfaction. There were several aspects of it that disturbed him—quite apart from the major problem of the fingerprints, which still had to be sorted out. That call from Edinburgh had come at such a very convenient time for him—*and* by previous arrangement—*and* after the need for punctuality had been earlier stressed to Whybrow. All pure chance, no doubt—but singularly fortunate for Otway. A transferred charge call, too—perfectly reasonable, but it *had* helped to establish the facts of the call beyond dispute.

Then, of course, there was the crucial point that Xanthe Otway had happened to ring the supervisor and discover that Lumsden's receiver was off just when she did. It was that that had fixed the upper limit of the murder time—as Otway himself had been quick to stress. "It must all have been over by then," he'd said. Without that call from Xanthe, the alibi would have been infinitely weaker. The medical report by itself wouldn't have provided conclusive proof of the time of death. Still—luck again, no doubt. After all, if reporting the phone out of order had been part of some deep plot, Xanthe could easily have gone out to a box and phoned the supervisor from there—without giving her name or becoming identifiable. . . . Also, Otway *had* volunteered the information about trying to ring Lumsden and calling the supervisor. He'd been completely open about it.

And yet . . .

Grant's thoughts turned to another nagging little matter—Otway's behavior over his projected journey to the north. It seemed clear that, at least as early as Saturday, he'd thought it very probable that he'd go to Edinburgh, or he wouldn't have bought a ticket and booked a sleeper. So why had he delayed until Sunday afternoon before ringing Lumsden and canceling his regular visit? It wasn't that he'd been waiting for Whybrow's report before ringing, because at that time Whybrow had still not reported. The point had no obvious bearing on the validity of the alibi—but Grant found it a bit puzzling. He must remember to ask Otway for an explanation. Of course, it was quite possible he was making too much of it. Otway could just have been rather remiss. Or undecided what to do. He could have had it in mind to pay a quick visit to Radlett late in the evening if Whybrow reported that the pictures weren't worth his inspection—and then, through tiredness perhaps, decided in the afternoon to call the visit off anyway. There could be many explanations. And, again, there'd been no attempt by Otway to conceal the facts of the cancellation. He'd been completely open about that, too.

Indeed, Grant had to admit, he'd been completely open about everything. He hadn't stumbled or hesitated or prevaricated. He'd offered reasonable grounds for all his actions. His manner throughout had been that of an innocent man. He'd been startled, affronted —but he'd never looked guilty. He hadn't had his alibi all ready, as a man depending on it might well have done—he'd remembered Whybrow's call only under pressure. What was more—and Grant had been particularly impressed by this—he'd rejected a perfectly good chance to account for the fingerprints. He could so easily have said yes to the inspector's question whether he'd taken the photograph and glass out of the frame when he'd handled it the previous week. He could have given some reason, however unlikely it might have seemed—and after that nothing could have been proved against him. But he'd impatiently brushed the suggestion aside. That, surely, was the act of a man with a clear conscience. . . . The fact was that he'd looked truthful and sounded truthful—and now, over the vital telephone call, he'd been proved truthful.

Yet there *were* all those coincidences. . . .

Grant went over in his mind once again his findings in connection with that call: Point one—it had been established beyond any doubt that the call had been put in by Whybrow at seven thirty, and taken at Otway's house. Point two—the fact of a two-way conversation between two men had been confirmed by three independent sources. Point three—Whybrow had said he'd talked to Otway. Point four—every answer Grant had got from every source had been consistent with the others. Not a single suspicious circumstance had emerged. Was there any loophole? Was there any way in which this conversation could have been faked?

Grant could think of only one possibility—and that bordered on fantasy. Suppose, he thought, that Otway's end of the conversation had somehow been recorded and used with the connivance both of Xanthe Otway and Whybrow. Was that feasible? A conversation carefully rehearsed beforehand by Otway and Whybrow, with Otway's part of the dialogue recorded on tape, and Whybrow filling in the gaps live from Scotland, and Xanthe working the machine at home? Just feasible, perhaps, in theory . . . But terribly tricky to operate, to time exactly. And always the possibility of a hitch, a breakdown, a mistake in handling. If anyone *had* been prepared to risk his neck with such a device, he would hardly have done it at a public counter with a receptionist standing by—a witness to any oddity. He'd have made sure of some quiet phone, where it wouldn't have mattered if the voice hadn't sounded right.

The voice . . . Grant suddenly remembered that the line hadn't been too good. According to Whybrow, anyway—the operator had seemed to find it all right. A poor line—that was intriguing. But Whybrow would hardly have admitted it was bad if he'd been conniving with Otway in a voice deception. . . . He'd have said it was fine. That really ruled him out. Anyway, there wasn't the slightest reason to suspect Whybrow's good faith. There wasn't an iota of evidence to suggest that he'd have joined Otway in a conspiracy to murder—or that Otway would have wanted or dared to bribe him to. In fact, if it hadn't been for those fingerprints, Grant knew that he wouldn't have been considering such a wild improbability for a second—he'd have accepted Otway's alibi without question, and looked elsewhere for the murderer.

The fingerprints . . . Well, if the alibi was sound the fingerprints obviously couldn't be. They were going to be a headache—but there *had* to be some explanation of them, that didn't involve Otway's guilt. Clearly, the only thing to do now was to take another look at the exhibits. . . .

15

Grant and Dawson sat with the evidence in front of them—the photograph frame with its picture, the fragments of broken glass from the studio floor, and the separate piece with the fingerprints on it. This, like some cherished specimen, now lay on cotton wool in a box of its own.

Grant picked it out with a pair of tweezers and took his first good look at it. It was a corner piece, with its right angle intact. One of its straight edges was about three inches long, the other two inches. The broken diagonal edge had a bulge outward. The dusted prints were plainly visible, on both sides.

"I suppose it does belong with the rest?" Dawson said.

The same question had been in Grant's mind. He compared it for color and thickness with one of the other pieces. They seemed alike. He started to poke around among the fragments, looking for one with an edge that corresponded with the broken edge of the fingerprint piece. He tried several, without success. Dawson watched the jigsaw effort with interest, scanning the bits. "Here, try this, sir," he said, picking out a piece. Grant tried it, and it made a perfect join.

"Well, that's one thing settled," Grant said.

He turned his attention to the photograph frame. It was about nine inches long by seven wide and consisted of four narrow strips of polished oak joined at the corners and backed by a piece of plywood held in position by small, swiveling clips. A hinged flap, on which the frame was intended to rest at a slight angle, had been broken as a result of the fall. One piece of glass was still held in place against the left side of the frame, between the oak strip and the plywood.

"Odd that that was the only bit to stay in," Dawson said. "I'd have expected the center of the glass to shatter and the rest to be held in all round."

Grant nodded. "So would I. . . ." He examined the frame more closely, testing the tightness of the glass that was still in. "If it had fallen on one of its edges, the bits at the top might have been jolted out—but hardly the others. . . ."

"If it had fallen on one of its edges, sir, I don't see why the flap should have broken."

"That's a point. . . . M'm—this begins to get interesting. . . ."

"And here's another odd thing," Dawson said. "If a sheet of glass had been in a photograph frame for years, wouldn't you expect to find some mark along its sides—a dust line?" He pointed to the fingerprint piece. "This is absolutely clean."

Grant opened the frame, took out the photograph, and examined the inside of the oak strips where the glass had pressed against them. They were dusty. He removed the piece of glass that had been held in place. Like all the other bits, it was clean.

For a moment, he sat frowning at it. It was a corner piece, about an inch wide at its right angle and about six inches long. The broken bottom end looked as though a small bite had been taken out of it. Grant started to rummage again among the fragments on the table, looking for one with a matching break. He found it almost at once. This, too, was a corner piece. Now they had one complete side of the glass. . . .

It didn't look right, even at a casual glance. With a sheet of paper, Grant measured the length of the side. Then he applied the paper to the inside of the frame.

Grimly, he looked at Dawson. "That was a good notion of yours about the dust line," he said. "This glass was never in the frame. It's half an inch too long. You know, Sergeant, I think this is going to be quite a case."

16

While Dawson packed the exhibits in a bag, Grant rang up Otway at the shop. He had some news, he said, that would probably come as a relief, and he'd be glad if they could meet at once. Otway said if the news was good he'd like his wife to hear it too, so why not meet at his flat? A few minutes later, the two policemen left for Chelsea.

Otway was already at the flat when they got there. With a cheerful "Come on in" he took them into the sitting room. Xanthe Otway, very elegant in a bronze satin housecoat, was smoking a cigarette in a long holder. Grant said, "Good morning, Mrs. Otway," and introduced Sergeant Dawson.

Xanthe acknowledged them coldly.

"After what happened at the shop yesterday," Grant said, "I

thought I'd better come along right away and set your minds at rest."

Xanthe's manner became even more frigid. "Our minds *have* been at rest."

"Oh, come off it, Xanthe," Otway said. "You know we didn't sleep a wink."

She ignored that. "I think it was absolutely outrageous to suggest what you did, Inspector. How *could* you? About George, of all people! When you knew he and John were such friends . . ."

Grant was unabashed. "If the evidence seems to point in a certain direction, Mrs. Otway, suspicion follows inevitably. It's a situation I have to live with."

"Well, I think it's quite disgraceful. . . ."

"Anyway," Otway said, "what's the position now? Did you check the telephone call?"

"I checked it, Mr. Otway, and I accept that Mr. Whybrow made it at seven thirty and that you took it."

"I should think so," Xanthe said.

"And what about the fingerprints?"

"Ah—well, there we've made a discovery. . . ." Grant opened his bag and took out the exhibits. "It appears that the glass we found in the studio—including the piece with your prints on it— didn't in fact come out of the photograph frame. It's the wrong size. I'll show you. . . ." He put the frame on the table and fitted the two corner pieces of glass together alongside it. "You see. . . ."

Otway stared down at it in bewilderment. "But I don't understand. What does it mean?"

"Well," Grant said, "it looks to me as though someone—presumably the murderer—had a sheet of glass with your fingerprints on it, which he took with him to the studio and substituted for the one already there. I can't think of any other explanation."

"You mean he *knew!* To make it look as though I did it!"

"That's what it seems like. He broke the glass—or, of course, he may have taken it already broken—and scattered it around, giving the impression that it had come out of the holder. He fitted one piece into a corner to strengthen the impression—that's where we found this bit. . . . He probably used gloves, in order not to leave prints of his own. And no doubt he took the original glass away with him."

"Well, I'm damned! A ruddy frame-up!"

"That's about it," Grant said.

"So *that* was why the piece of glass with the prints was left on the desk!"

Grant looked a bit sheepish. "Yes—I'm afraid my reconstruction yesterday was a little wide of the mark."

"The murderer just wanted to draw attention to it?"

"Not *just* that . . . He obviously had to make it appear that that piece had been picked up, otherwise there'd have been nothing to account for the prints that were on it. . . . Not too satisfactory from his point of view—but he had to do the best he could."

"It all sounds pretty clumsy to me." Otway was still staring at the exhibits. "The wrong-sized glass . . ."

"I don't suppose he had any choice about that, either," Grant said. "Even if he'd known the exact size of the photograph frame, which he may not have done, he'd have had to make do with the sheet of glass he'd got hold of. . . . Probably he thought the slight difference in size wouldn't matter, anyway—and he could easily have been right. If you hadn't had an alibi that forced us to go into the whole question of the prints again, it's quite on the cards that no one would have troubled to fit the pieces of glass together. The frame was there, and the glass was there—who would have doubted that they belonged to each other?"

"That's true. . . ." Otway was looking very troubled. "Well, the whole thing's extremely unpleasant, I must say. . . ."

"It's absolutely monstrous," Xanthe said hotly.

Otway was less indignant—but more worried. "Someone must have had it in for me in a big way."

"Not necessarily in a big way," Grant said. "The murderer can't be exactly fond of you—but I doubt if he picked on you merely out of spite. His chief concern would have been to deflect suspicion from himself—and the best way he could do that was to choose someone to frame who seemed to have a strong motive. You qualified."

"Yes—I see. . . ."

There was a little silence.

"Well," Grant said more briskly, "our job now is to find out who this man is."

"I can't think how, Inspector."

"Oh, I'd say we'd quite a bit to go on, Mr. Otway. Let's start with this piece of glass—which I'm sure you've been thinking about. Your prints are on it, so you must have handled it at some time. Almost certainly when it was still part of an unbroken sheet. Now where might you have done that?"

"In the shop, I should imagine—I can't think of anywhere else. We keep quite a lot of glass there."

Grant nodded. "Yes, I saw you did."

Otway picked up one of the fragments and examined it. "About this quality and thickness, too."

"What about the size?"

"We've got most sizes. I'd have to look."

"*Do* you sometimes handle the glass there?"

"Oh, yes . . . I don't recall any particular occasion—but then I handle so much stuff."

"Do you ever serve in the shop yourself?"

"Occasionally—when there's a big rush."

The inspector gave a satisfied grunt. "In that case, I think we may be making progress. Now, could something like this have happened?—just one of many possibilities. A man comes into the shop. He's planning to murder John Lumsden. He knows you, or about you, and he'd like to put the blame on you if he can. The shop is busy, and you are serving. Some customer is asking you if you've a sheet of glass to fit a frame he's brought along—a frame about the same size as this one here. You pick out a sheet and try it—holding it by the bottom right-hand corner between your thumb and two fingers. It doesn't fit and you put it down again. Our man sees you do it. He realizes that this is his opportunity. When your attention is on something else, he buys the sheet of glass from one of your assistants and takes it away with him. And he has your fingerprints. Would something like that be possible?"

Otway gave a thoughtful nod. "I should think so. Yes, that could account for the prints. Very clever of you, Inspector. But it still leaves the field pretty wide open, doesn't it?'

"Not as wide as you might think," Grant said. "Don't forget we know other things about this man—a great many things. . . . In the first place, he must have stood to benefit from Lumsden's death himself, in some way, or he wouldn't have wanted to murder him. Secondly, he must have known that you'd appear to have a strong motive, or he wouldn't have thought of framing you. Thirdly, he must have known that there was a photograph frame in the studio —and at least its approximate size. Fourthly, he must have known all about the domestic arrangements at Lumsden's house—about Mrs. Bowen's Sunday-night outings, and your regular visits. In fact, he must have been an intimate of the family. . . . There can't be many men who meet all those requirements. . . . Tell me, Mr. Otway, did Michael Ransley ever come to your shop?"

Xanthe broke in sharply. "Heavens, you can't suspect Mike. That's almost more fantastic than suspecting George."

"Why do you say that, Mrs. Otway?"

"Well—to kill your own uncle!"

Grant snorted. "It wouldn't be the first time it had happened," he said, "not by a long chalk. . . ." He turned again to Otway. "Did he ever come to the shop?"

"Now and again," Otway said. "But . . ."

"What did he come for?"

"Always to have a picture framed. John was very generous with his canvases and he gave several to Mike. And Mike always brought them along to us. . . ."

"When was the last time this happened?"

"Oh, quite a while back . . ." Otway looked at Xanthe. "Do you remember, darling?"

"No, I don't," Xanthe said. "And I think the whole idea's preposterous."

"Well, Mr. Otway?"

"I'm trying to remember. . . . I think it must have been that still life—about a couple of months ago."

"Were you at the shop when Mr. Ransley called?"

"Yes—I helped him find a suitable frame."

"Were you serving in the shop?"

"As a matter of fact, I think I was. There were a lot of customers that day."

"H'm . . . Tell me, how well do you get on with Mr. Ransley?"

"Quite well," Otway said. "We don't see a lot of each other, though."

"When did you last see him?"

"I think it must have been that time when he came to the shop."

"As long as that . . . Do you like him?"

"Yes, I do. As I say, I don't know him well—we move in different circles. He's a very clever chap—knows a lot about politics, world affairs. . . . I rather admire him."

"Does he like you?"

"Well . . ." Again Otway looked at Xanthe.

"I want the truth, Mr. Otway. Straight, if you don't mind."

Otway shrugged. "To be honest, I'm not sure that he does like me. I've always had the feeling that he considered me a bit of an upstart—you know, getting on so well with his uncle—and then this will business . . ."

"Did he ever say anything to that effect?"

"Oh, no—it was just something in his manner—a bit disapproving . . . But that doesn't mean he'd have tried to frame me for a murder he'd committed—and I'm damned sure he didn't. . . ."

"So am I," Xanthe said.

Grant gave a slightly sour smile. "Loyalty's a fine thing—but I'm afraid I have to go where the facts lead me. . . ." He got to his feet.

"What are you going to do?" Otway asked.

"Well, first I'd like to come back to the shop with you, and check on the size of the glass sheets there. If we find there are some similar to the one that was used, then I'd like a word with your assistants. Do they know Mr. Ransley?"

Otway looked doubtful. "Peter does—Peter Carruthers. . . . I'm not sure about the others."

"Well," Grant said, "let's go and see."

17

The shop was having a quiet period when they arrived, and they took advantage of it to get through the investigation quickly. Otway went straight to the shelf with the piles of glass sheets on it and ran his eye over them, glancing down for comparison at the frame that Grant was holding. In a moment, he'd pulled one of the sheets out. "How about this?"

Grant took it from him, and applied a tape measure to its longer side. It was exactly the same length as the side he'd reconstructed from the broken pieces. The width was approximately the same as that of the frame. In thickness and in color it was identical with the broken bits.

"Looks as though you were right," Otway said. "It *could* have come from here. But that doesn't mean . . ."

Grant interrupted him. "Let's see what your assistants have to say, shall we?"

Otway called them over, one by one, and introduced them. The interviews didn't take very long. Carruthers, the right-hand man, said he knew Mr. Ransley well and was quite sure he'd never served him with a sheet of glass. The second assistant, a young fellow named Miles, didn't know Ransley and didn't recall him even when Otway described him. He *might* have served him with a sheet of glass, he said, but he'd no recollection. The girl also didn't know Ransley, though she thought she vaguely remembered him from the description. She said she recalled selling a small sheet of glass to some man not so long ago, but she couldn't remember when and she'd no idea now what he'd looked like. Grant urged her to think hard, giving her time, encouraging her—but it was quite useless. She served so many people, she said, that it was difficult to keep faces in mind. . . .

Otway turned to Grant with undisguised relief. "Well, there you are, Inspector. . . . There's nothing at all to suggest it was Mike who bought the glass—if anyone did. . . ."

"There's nothing at all to suggest it wasn't," Grant said. "The evidence is inconclusive—which means we'll have to make other inquiries. Sergeant, we'd better fix up a session with Mr. Ransley."

18

The two detectives called on Michael Ransley by appointment at seven o'clock that evening. His Barnet flat, in contrast to the Otways', proved to be a modest, even austere apartment. Ransley himself was very much as Dawson had described him—a slight but well-proportioned man in his early thirties, about five foot six in height, carefully dressed in a suit of clerical gray, and with a quiet, reserved manner. He had, Grant thought, little resemblance to his dead uncle—the only obvious similarity was a rather high forehead. With his dark eyes, his pale, clean-cut face and his air of rather watchful intelligence he was interesting looking rather than handsome. A greater contrast to the extrovert and positive Otway could hardly have been imagined.

Dawson introduced the inspector, and Ransley found seats for them. Then he sat looking at Grant, waiting for him to begin.

"It's about the death of your uncle, of course, that I wanted to talk to you," Grant said. "I'd intended to come and see you before —but I've been rather involved with Mr. Otway. . . . At one time, it seemed possible that he might have been concerned in the murder."

"Really?" Ransley's flat tone showed no trace of surprise—only, Grant thought, an extreme wariness. It was going to be hard to get helpful reactions from him—even to deliberately startling statements.

"Yes," Grant said. "For a while things looked bad for him. But it turns out that he couldn't have been there—he has a complete alibi. So we've had to rule him out."

"Oh . . . I'm glad to hear it."

"Now I have some questions to put to you, Mr. Ransley."

Ransley gave a slight nod. "I assumed this wasn't a social call, Inspector. . . . Go ahead—I'm listening."

"You know, I think, that you are your uncle's co-heir with Mr. Otway?"

"I know he told me about two years ago that he was making a will to that effect."

"And you knew he was a wealthy man?"

"I didn't know whether he was wealthy or not."

"Oh . . ." Grant paused. Then he began again. "Did you know that his late wife belonged to a well-to-do family?"

Ransley hesitated. "Yes . . . I knew that. . . ."

"Then it would be reasonable, wouldn't it, to suppose that she probably had money of her own?"

"Reasonable, yes . . ."

"Which, in the normal course of events, she would leave to her husband if she died first?"

"I suppose so. . . ."

"You knew, also, the circumstances in which your uncle lived in recent years? You knew that he had an expensive house in Radlett, that he owned a cottage in Suffolk, that he employed a housekeeper, that he had a taste for antique furniture, ran a two-thousand-pound car, and traveled a good deal?"

"I—well, yes."

"Putting all these things together, you could hardly have supposed that his estate would be negligible?"

"I didn't say that, Inspector. What I said was that I didn't know he was *wealthy*. These things are relative."

"They are indeed, Mr. Ransley. Would you care to give me some idea of your own financial position?"

"I earn just over fifteen hundred a year."

"In the Foreign Office, I understand."

"Yes."

"And your salary might rise in the end to—two or three thousand?"

"Something of that order."

"Have you any private means?"

"Nothing to speak of."

"So that being the co-heir of a man in Lumsden's position could hardly have been a matter of indifference to you?"

"Not of indifference, no."

Grant sighed. "Well, I'm glad we've struggled through to an agreement on something, Mr. Ransley! It may interest you to know that your uncle actually left about two hundred thousand pounds —of which, unless something untoward arises, you will eventually enjoy half."

"I see."

"I suppose," Grant said, "that in the Foreign Office you're trained to conceal your feelings."

"It sometimes helps, Inspector."

"H'm . . . Well, let's continue. Did you know that your uncle intended to marry his housekeeper, Mrs. Bowen?"

"No—I didn't."

"Did you expect he would?"

"I can't say I thought about it."

"Really? I understood from Mr. Otway that, in conversation with him, you prophesied it."

"I did nothing of the sort."

"That was his clear recollection."

"Then he was mistaken," Ransley said. "I never discussed it with him."

Grant regarded him dubiously. "Well, perhaps we can sort that out later. I certainly find it strange that the idea of marriage should never have occurred to you. Mr. Otway himself wasn't at all surprised at the news—he said that Mrs. Bowen and Mr. Lumsden got on excellently together and that marriage was obviously in the cards. . . ."

"Otway saw much more of my uncle than I did," Ransley said. "I haven't been to his house for quite a while."

"H'm . . . Of course, Mr. Ransley, if you *had* known that your uncle was very wealthy, and that he was planning to marry his housekeeper, and that he might therefore change his will, you would have had—in theory—a good motive for wanting him dead."

"That's ridiculous. I was very fond of my uncle."

"You were?"

"Certainly."

"Well, of course, if you were, you obviously wouldn't have wanted him dead. Let's look into it a little, shall we? According to Mrs. Bowen, you used to visit the house quite a lot."

"Yes . . ."

"But you now tell me you haven't done so for some time. When, in fact, did you last see Mr. Lumsden?"

"About—oh, two months ago, I suppose."

"Two months . . . You were fond of him, you got on well with him, you once visited him a lot, you live within easy distance of him—but you haven't seen him for two months. Why the change, Mr. Ransley?"

Ransley was silent.

"Well?" Grant said sharply. "What's your answer?"

Ransley shrugged. "It's really quite simple, Inspector. I met a girl—actually, I'm going to marry her. So my time became rather occupied."

"I see. But surely you wanted to take this girl along to meet your uncle?"

"I wanted to, of course, and I was going to. We just hadn't got around to it yet."

"Did you tell your uncle you were planning to get married? Did you write to him, or telephone him?"

"Well, no. . . . One doesn't announce these things immediately."

"I rather thought one did. Especially to a relative one was fond of, a close relative, a relative from whom one was going to inherit a lot of money. . . ."

Ransley said nothing. He was beginning to look very uncomfortable.

Grant said, "Who is your fiancée, Mr. Ransley?"

"She—she's a girl who works at the B.B.C."

"What's her name?"

"Irma Felding."

"Irma Felding . . . Is she foreign?"

"She's German."

"Oh . . ." There was a long, reflective pause. Then Grant said, "Mr. Ransley, when I was in your uncle's studio I saw a picture, an unpleasantly vivid picture, of Belsen concentration camp. . . . You know it, I expect."

"Yes . . ."

"Did Mr. Lumsden paint it on the site, do you happen to know?"

"I believe he made some drawings for it there."

"He must have done them soon after the camp was entered."

"The same day, I think."

"The horrors of the place obviously made a deep impression on him."

"Yes."

"So much so that afterward he couldn't bear any Germans— isn't that right, Mr. Ransley? Wasn't that why you didn't tell him about your fiancée? Isn't that why you haven't visited his house for two months?"

Ransley hesitated—then gave a reluctant nod. "He was very prejudiced. He talked as though all Germans were butchers, monsters. . . . Even the children . . . I know he'd seen terrible things, I can understand how he got that way—but I thought it better not to meet him. I simply wanted to avoid unpleasantness."

"Just unpleasantness? Not being cut out of his will?"

"That didn't enter into it."

"Didn't he wonder what was keeping you away so long? Didn't he ask you?"

"He rang me once or twice—but I made excuses. . . ."

"H'm . . . And in spite of all this, you still say you were fond of your uncle!"

"This was a blind spot of his. Until I met Irma, what he thought about Germans didn't worry me."

"But afterward you resented his attitude?"

"Well, wouldn't you?"

"I'm not criticizing you for that, Mr. Ransley—only for withholding the truth from me about your relationship with him. It's quite clear to me now that at the time he died you weren't at all fond of him. . . . Well, let's move on. . . . In the days when you used to visit him, I take it you became familiar with his domestic arrangements?"

"I wouldn't say that."

"You wouldn't? All right, we'll take it a step at a time. You knew he had a housekeeper!"

"Of course."

"No doubt you spoke to her sometimes?"

"Naturally."

"Did she ever talk to you about herself?"

"Occasionally."

"Did you know she had a sister?"

"Yes."

"Did you know she always went to see her sister on Sunday evenings?"

"I knew she often did."

"Did you know the hour at which she often set out? You might just as well be frank with me—I can check all these things with her."

"I knew she usually went about seven."

"Leaving your uncle to his own devices?"

"No—Otway always went to play chess with him on Sundays."

"Oh, you knew that, too?"

"Yes."

"Did you know what time he usually arrived?"

"I suppose it varied."

"I'm told your uncle was a stickler for keeping to a schedule?"

"Well, he was, rather. . . ."

"So perhaps the time didn't vary?"

"I don't know."

"If you'd wanted to know, you could easily have found out, couldn't you?"

"I suppose I could."

"Good! Well, now, Mr. Ransley, I'm going to be a lot franker with you than you've been with me. This murder was committed between the hours of seven and eight o'clock on Sunday evening by a man who had no friendly feeling for Lumsden, who stood to gain by his death, and who was familiar with his household arrangements. There was a bit of a struggle before the killing, and broken glass which appeared to have come from a photograph frame was scattered around. One piece of the glass was found to have Mr. Otway's fingerprints on it—on both sides. . . ."

Ransley stared. "But surely, in that case . . ."

Grant shook his head. "As I told you, Mr. Otway has an alibi. There's fully substantiated evidence that he was taking a telephone call at his home at the material time. There's also evidence that the glass with the prints on it was never in the frame. The probability is that it was part of a sheet purchased from Mr. Otway's shop. It seems that someone who didn't expect him to have an alibi planted it in the studio with the deliberate intention of incriminating him. Obviously the murderer . . ."

"Are you suggesting that I did that?" Ransley said coldly.

"Shall we say that I'm exploring the possibility? In a number of respects, you certainly seem to qualify. . . . I'm told you visited Mr. Otway's shop about two months ago."

"Well?"

"To get a picture framed, wasn't it?"

"That's right. A still life with fruit."

"Where is it now?"

"In a cupboard."

"Oh—you didn't hang it? Don't you like your uncle's work?"

"I didn't like that particular thing."

"Then why did you bother to have it framed? Was it because you wanted an excuse to go to the shop?"

"Of course not . . . I didn't want to offend him, that's all."

"That must have been before you decided to break off relations with him."

"Yes, just before . . . It was the last contact we had, apart from the phone."

"I see. . . . Now when you visited the shop, I gather you saw Mr. Otway."

Ransley frowned. "I don't remember doing so. . . ."

"Otway says you did. He says he looked after you."

"My recollection is that an assistant served me. I don't think he was there. . . ."

"A lot of your recollections seem a bit hazy, Mr. Ransley. Let's suppose you did see him. Let's suppose that you saw him showing a sheet of glass to a customer. In that case, you might well have had the opportunity to go off with the glass—and his fingerprints. And use them later . . . Pure hypothesis, of course—but possible?"

"Nothing of the sort happened, Inspector—I can tell you that. I wouldn't have dreamed of killing my uncle—and if I had I'd never have framed George. It's a monstrous suggestion. . . ."

"H'm . . . What are your relations with Mr. Otway?"

"They're—very good."

"Close?"

"Friendly."

"You visit him at his house, no doubt?"

"Well, no . . ."

"You don't? Have you met his wife?"

"I—I've met her once."

"Just once?"

"It isn't that sort of relationship. It's—well, just between George and me."

"A confidential relationship?"

"You could call it that."

"No doubt you told him about your fiancée, then?"

"Well—no . . ."

"Why not?"

"I didn't want it mentioned to my uncle."

"Would he have mentioned it if you'd asked him not to? Didn't you trust him?"

"It just didn't occur to me to tell him."

"I see. . . . But you definitely liked him?"

"Yes."

"It's odd—Mr. Otway gave me the impression that you didn't. He thought you disapproved of him, as an upstart who'd wormed his way into your uncle's affections and collared half your inheritance."

"I'm very surprised. He'd no reason to think that."

"It isn't true?"

"Of course not."

"What exactly do you like about Mr. Otway?"

Ransley hesitated. "Well—he's good-humored—cheerful—a carefree sort of chap. . . ."

"Yes?" Grant said. "Go on. . . ."

"He's—he's got quite a flair for pictures. Smart at his job. . . ."

"So's a good burglar," Grant said. "I'd hardly call this a paean of praise so far."

"It's difficult to put into words. . . . He's—well, he's just likable, that's all."

"H'm! I'd expect a much better testimonial from any friend of mine, I must say. Quite frankly, Mr. Ransley, I don't believe you like him at all. My impression is that you dislike him—and that you've kept away from him as much as possible for that reason."

"It's not true," Ransley said. Beads of sweat had gathered on his forehead. He mopped at them delicately with a clean white handkerchief from his breast pocket.

"You find it warm in here?" Grant asked.

"A little."

"I'll open a window—let a bit of fresh air in!" He did so. Suddenly he swung round. "Mr. Ransley, where *were* you around seven o'clock on Sunday evening?"

Ransley was still mopping. All his earlier composure seemed to have gone. "I'm surprised you haven't asked me that before," he said.

"I've been waiting for you to tell me—and wondering why you didn't."

"Well," Ransley said, "actually, I was driving to Stone Cross Hospital."

"Oh? Why?"

"I was going to give some blood. I'm a registered donor."

"Are you?" Grant looked at him with the deepest suspicion. "Isn't Stone Cross Hospital very near your uncle's house?"

"Yes."

"How far away?"

"Oh—a couple of minutes' drive."

"And it's some distance from here. A quarter of an hour's drive?"

"About that."

"Do you usually go to Stone Cross to give blood?"

"No—but I had a telephone call. It's a bit complicated. . . ."

"Take your time, Mr. Ransley—I'm in no hurry."

"Well—I'd been playing golf in the afternoon, and I got home about five. I'd just had a bath when the phone rang and a woman said she was Sister something-or-other at Stone Cross Hospital and could I go along there and give some blood for an accident case. So of course I said I would—mine is a rare blood group and I've been called on before like that. She said that seven thirty would be the most convenient time for them, and though it wasn't too convenient for me I made the appointment. . . ." Ransley paused.

"And you kept it?" Grant asked.

"Oh, yes, I kept it. But when I got there, just before half past seven, I discovered that no one at the hospital knew anything at all about it. They hadn't got an accident case and they didn't need the blood and they hadn't rung up. The telephone call had been a hoax."

"I see," Grant said. He couldn't have sounded more skeptical. "Have you any idea who the hoaxer might have been?"

"None."

"Do many people know that you're a blood donor?"

"Quite a number, I should think. I haven't publicized it—but I haven't made a secret of it."

"Did this woman's voice seem at all familiar to you?"

"No."

"What was it like?"

Ransley frowned. "I find it hard to describe. . . . The line was rather bad."

"In what way?"

"It was sort of echoing. . . . I thought at the time that the Sister must be speaking from a large ward."

"Even so, you can surely tell me something about the voice? Was it high or low? Was it educated? Had it an accent?"

"It was rather high," Ransley said. "No special accent. A fairly normal sort of voice . . . I wasn't paying much attention to it at the time. Why should I?"

"H'm . . . Have you ever had any trouble with hoaxers before, Mr. Ransley?"

"No."

"Did you tell anyone that you'd had this call and were going to the hospital?"

"I told my fiancée. I'd arranged to spend the evening with her, and it meant I was going to be late."

"Anyone else?"

"No."

"Did you tell anyone about the hoax—afterward?"

"I told Irma, of course, later in the evening. No one else."

Grant nodded. "May I have your fiancée's address?"

"Forty-three, West Heath Avenue, Hampstead."

Grant made a note. "You didn't make any effort to trace the call, then?"

"No—I thought it was probably a local call—there didn't seem much chance of tracking it down."

"And you didn't think of mentioning the hoax to the police?"

Ransley shook his head. "It hardly seemed worth bothering them about."

"Not even after you'd heard about the murder? Didn't it strike you as at all strange that you'd been called to a hospital so near your uncle's, by a hoax call, at the very time he'd been killed?"

"Well, I did wonder about that. . . ."

"You could easily have mentioned the hoax to Sergeant Dawson when you saw him late on Sunday night."

"I was so shocked, Inspector, I didn't think of it."

"So in fact you did nothing about it, either then or later?"

"No . . ."

"H'm . . . Tell me, Mr. Ransley, how long have you been a blood donor?"

"About six months."

"What made you become one?"

"Actually, my uncle was talking about it one evening—he'd just read an article about how important it was. It seemed a fairly painless way of doing a bit of good."

"And of keeping on the right side of him?"

"You make all my motives seem bad."

"Didn't it occur to you, when this call was made, that if blood was wanted for an accident case it would be wanted at once and not in an hour or two?"

"I did think that was a bit odd," Ransley said, "but I supposed that they had some of the group on hand, and merely wanted some more. . . . One doesn't normally argue with hospitals."

The inspector grunted. "Well, now, I'd like a detailed timetable of your movements on Sunday evening. What time did you say you left for the hospital?"

"Just after seven."

"What car do you drive?"

"A Consul."

"Color?"

"Green."

"Have you had it long?"

"About two years."

"Where was it parked on Sunday—outside the flat?"

"No, a little way down the road. There wasn't room here."

"Did anyone see you leave here? Anyone we might get hold of?"

"Not that I know of."

"You didn't speak to anyone on your way out?"

"No."

"Did you stop for gas anywhere?"

"No."

"If the hospital is only fifteen minutes' drive from here, why did you allow yourself nearly half an hour for the trip?"

"It was a misty night—I didn't want to have to hurry."

"If you had hurried, you could have got to Radlett by seven fifteen?"

"Probably—but I didn't."

"Or even earlier, if you'd left *before* seven."

"I told you when I left."

"But there's no independent evidence on the point?"

"No . . ."

"What time did you leave the hospital?"

"About eight, I think."

"Did you drive straight to your fiancée's house?"

"Yes."

"And what time did you get there?"

"Just before half past eight."

"I see. . . ." Grant closed his notebook and sat silent for a while. "Well, it's all most interesting. . . . You realize, of course, that I've only your word for it that this telephone call was ever made?"

"I know."

"And that, if you *had* intended to kill your uncle on Sunday evening, you'd have needed some story like this. You'd have known you were bound to be asked where you'd been—and since there was always the chance that someone in Radlett might have seen and recognized you—or your car—you'd have needed a good explanation for being in the district. I don't doubt the hospital will confirm that you were there just before seven thirty—and that's as good a cover as you could expect."

"Well—those weren't the circumstances at all, Inspector. I've told you what happened—and it's the truth."

Grant looked hard at him. "If it is, it took you a long while to reach it—didn't it, Mr. Ransley?"

19

The policemen had a lot to consider and discuss now—too much to make a start worth while on a short car journey. As they sped toward Stone Cross, the inspector's thoughts were more on what the hospital might tell them than on the interview they'd just finished.

"You know," he said, as they turned in through the wrought-iron gates, "if the people here do confirm the times Ransley gave us—arrived seven thirty, left about eight—this could be a most illuminating visit."

"How so, sir?"

"Well, it'll mean that if he did kill Lumsden, he did it before he called here. And not very long before—because Kathie didn't leave Lumsden's house till seven. Perhaps just a few minutes before. . . . I'll be interested to hear what sort of state he was in when he got here."

Dawson nodded in the darkness. "Yes, that's quite a point, sir. . . ."

The hospital proved to be a small one. There was nobody in the porter's office at the entrance, so they went straight on in and asked a nurse to direct them to the Night Sister's room. She took them along herself, and they knocked and entered.

Once they had stated their business, the Night Sister—her name was Mackie—was briskly helpful. She had been on duty on Sunday also, it appeared; she remembered Ransley very well indeed, and was able to confirm at least a part of his story. He'd arrived, she said, about half past seven. He'd introduced himself, and said he'd come to give the blood they'd asked for, and explained about the afternoon telephone call. Sister Mackie had known nothing about it, and had made inquiries. She'd soon discovered that no such request had come from Stone Cross. Mr. Ransley had been quite certain he'd made no mistake about the name of the hospital, and they'd finally had to accept that the call had been a stupid hoax. He'd left her at about ten minutes to eight.

"What was your impression of him?" Grant asked. "Did he strike you as being quite genuine?"

Sister Mackie looked surprised. "Why, yes . . ."

"You had the feeling that he came here really expecting to give some blood?"

"I'd certainly no reason not to think so."

"What did he say when he found it was a hoax?"

"Well, he was rather put out. Anyone would have been—it wasn't a very nice thing to happen. But he took it very well, considering. I thought he was a pleasant young man."

"Did he seem at all agitated when he first came in? Before he found out about the hoax?"

"Agitated? No, I wouldn't say that. His hair was a bit disheveled and he was sweating a little. I assumed he'd been hurrying to keep the appointment."

"What about his clothes? Were they clean, tidy?"

"They looked all right."

"Was he wearing gloves?"

"He was carrying a pair."

"H'm . . . Well, thanks a lot, Sister. I'm much obliged to you. . . ."

As they were about to leave the hospital, Grant noticed that the porter was back in his cubby hole, drinking tea. He stopped and identified himself.

"Do you remember a Mr. Ransley coming here about half past seven last Sunday evening?" he asked. "A small, neat man—about thirty . . . Came to give some blood."

"Oh, yes, sir, I remember him," the porter said at once. "I sent him along to the Night Sister. There was some mistake about it, wasn't there?"

"That's right. . . . Tell me—when he first came in, did he seem at all upset?"

"Well, it's odd you should ask that, sir—as a matter of fact, he did. Really shaky, he was, and pale as anything. Said he'd just seen a cat run over."

"*Did* he!" Grant looked very grim. "Thank you. . . ."

20

They stopped at the first telephone booth they came to. Dawson stood by the door, propping it open. The inspector rammed coins into the box as though he were loading a gun.

"This is Grant again," he said without ceremony, as Ransley answered. "I've just been talking to the porter at Stone Cross. . . . What's all this I hear about a cat?"

There was a moment of silence. Then Ransley said, "Oh, yes—a cat was run over. . . . Just in front of me."

"When did this happen?"

"Not long before I got to the hospital."

"*Where* did it happen?"

"I'm afraid I can't tell you the exact spot. It was on that straight stretch of country road just before Radlett."

"There are nearly two miles of that," Grant said sharply. "Surely you've some idea how far along you were?"

"I'm sorry. It was very dark and misty on Sunday. I really don't know. . . ."

"All right—give me some details of this tragedy."

"A car was in front of me," Ransley said, "going in the same direction. A cat shot out of the hedge—and the car hit it. . . ."

"Did the car stop?"

"No."

"Did you see what make of car it was?"

"No."

"Did *you* stop?"

"Yes."

"What did you do?"

"I walked up to the cat. It was writhing horribly. I'd have tried to finish it off but I didn't know how. Then it suddenly died."

"What sort of cat was it?"

"A tabby."

"What did you do with its body?"

"I put it in a ditch. Really, Inspector, what on earth has this got to do with the case?"

"It could have plenty to do with it," Grant snapped. "I'm told you arrived at the hospital in quite a state."

"Oh—I see. Well, I wouldn't say I was in a state. I was a bit upset."

"You must be a very softhearted man."

"I suppose I am."

"Like Crippen."

"I beg your pardon?"

"Skip it! What was it that upset you, exactly? Was there a lot of blood?"

"There wasn't any. It was just that I saw the cat in my headlights after it had been knocked over—and it was in agony. It turned two complete somersaults in the air, all twisted up. I've never seen anything like it. . . ."

Grant flung the receiver down. "Blasted fellow!" he muttered. He stamped out of the box. "Now I suppose we'll have to turn out the whole county force to look for a dead tabby in two miles of ditch! No wonder the police are short-handed!"

21

Still simmering, Grant headed the car for Hampstead and the last job of the evening—a call on Michael Ransley's fiancée. They reached West Heath Avenue just before ten. Number 43 proved to be a three-story Victorian building converted into flats. Irma Felding had the one at the top—and she was at home. She showed no surprise when Grant announced himself. "Come in, please," she said in a friendly voice.

"You were expecting us?" Grant asked.

"Yes . . . Mike telephoned and said he thought you might want to see me." She was a girl in her early twenties, about five foot four, with a luscious figure, large wide-open blue eyes, and a lot of very fair hair piled on top of her head. Her accent was noticeably foreign and rather engaging. A very different type, Grant thought, from the other woman in the case, Xanthe Otway—but, in her own way, just as striking.

"It was thoughtful of Mr. Ransley to prepare you," Grant said, with an irony that appeared to be lost on the girl. "What exactly did he tell you?"

"He said you had wanted his help in your inquiries about his uncle," Irma said. "And that you might wish to ask me some questions, too."

"He didn't go into details?"

"No."

"H'm . . ." Grant gave her a long, hard stare. She looked a picture of childlike innocence. Her expression was a little bewildered, a little troubled—a not-quite-used-to-your-country, not-quite-used-to-murder expression, Grant thought. Appealing, disarming . . . But was it innocence—or was it guile? How ignorant was she? If Ransley *had* killed his uncle, it was quite possible that she'd been in on it from the beginning, that she'd helped him plot the murder. . . . Alternatively, he could have done it on his own, and kept the crime a secret from her. . . . Or, if he hadn't done it, he might still have chosen to say nothing to her about his embarrassing involvement. She could know all, or hardly anything. . . . Grant debated whether to tell her brutally that her boy friend was his number-one suspect—to throw the evidence at her and see how she reacted. But she looked so defenseless that he decided to hold his fire.

"There are a few questions," he said. "You'll understand, I'm sure, that in these cases we have to check everything, over and over. . . ."

"I do understand," she said.

"First, then, about this telephone call that was supposed to have come from the hospital . . ." Item by item, Grant went over Ransley's story with her, probing for any weakness, any discrepancy. But he found none. Mike had rung her up, Irma said, at about half past five on Sunday afternoon to tell her he had to go to the hospital. She'd been disappointed, because she'd been expecting him at her flat at half past six, but she hadn't been exactly surprised because a similar thing had happened once before. He'd actually arrived about half past eight, and he'd told her then about the hoax. He'd been rather angry and upset about it. They'd discussed it for a while, wondering who the woman could have been, realizing it must have been someone who'd known Mike was a donor. Irma had teased him a little, saying it must have been one of his earlier girl friends paying him back for desertion. Then she'd got supper, and they'd opened a bottle of wine and hadn't bothered any more. . . .

"Did he tell you about the cat?" Grant asked.

"The cat?" Irma's nose wrinkled, rather charmingly. "Oh, yes, poor boy . . . That had upset him too. He is very kind."

"Did he say where it had happened?"

"No."

"Or when?"

"No . . ." Irma looked surprised. "Is it so important?"

"It's hard to know what's important, Miss Felding. Now when did you first hear that Mr. Lumsden had been killed?"

"Mike rang me up early on Monday morning—before eight o'clock."

"What did he say about it?"

"What could he say? He was shocked. I think he could hardly believe it. He was worried, too, because he thought it would distress me. I was distressed, of course—it is a terrible thing to happen in a family—but I was distressed for him. He worries very much, even over small things, and this was not small. He is a very sensitive man, very—what is the word?—vulnerable. . . . He has been so unhappy ever since—it has been a great cloud over us."

"It must have been," Grant said. "I take it Mr. Ransley was very fond of his uncle?"

Irma hesitated. "I think he was quite fond of him—as an uncle. . . . It is not, after all, a very close relationship."

The inspector grunted. "Well, now, Miss Felding, perhaps you'd tell me a little about yourself. . . . How old are you?"

"I'm twenty-six."

"And you're working at the B.B.C.—is that right?"

Irma nodded.

"What are you doing there?"

"It is a kind of exchange arrangement, in connection with Eurovision. Really, I am learning. I thought I would go back to Germany and work on television there—but now I think I will be married and stay here." She smiled. "Perhaps I will continue to work, though —it is very interesting. . . ."

"What part of Germany do you come from?"

"From the Rhineland—from Coblenz."

"Are your parents alive?"

"Oh, yes."

"What does your father do?"

Irma's face clouded. "He does very little now. He is not well."

"What *did* he do?"

The cloud remained. "Until after the war, he was a judge."

"A *judge?* And then?"

Irma gave a little shrug. "During the war he was a Nazi—everyone had to be. It was a bad time. . . . Afterward, he was dismissed."

"I see. . . . When did you come over here, Miss Felding?"

"About eight months ago."

"And how long have you known Mr. Ransley?"

"About—three months."

"Where did you meet him?"

"At a party."

"When did you become engaged?"

"A week or two later."

"Weren't you surprised that he didn't introduce you to his uncle?"

"No—because he explained," Irma said. "I wanted to meet Mr. Lumsden—I thought perhaps I could make him like me a little—but Mike said better to wait, because he was so prejudiced. I was sorry—it seemed unfair. When the war ended I was only eight years old. Could I be guilty of anything?"

Grant wondered.

22

Back at the Yard there were one or two chores to be attended to before the two policemen could settle down to discuss the case against Ransley. Grant dealt with a query about the Lumsden inquest, and arranged with the county police to start a search next morning for a dead tabby cat. He also asked that inquiries should be made in the roads around Lumsden's house to see if anyone had noticed a green Consul parked on the murder evening anywhere except outside the hospital. Dawson, meanwhile, made a routine check with the telephone people to see if they had any record of a call to Ransley's number around the time of the alleged hoax. But they hadn't. If the call had been made, it had been dialed.

It was nearly eleven o'clock when Grant, relaxed with a pipe, finally said, "Well, Sergeant, what do you think? Did he, or didn't he?"

Dawson took a coin from his pocket, spun it, and slapped it on the back of his hand. "Seems he didn't, sir."

Grant smiled. "You'll have to do better than that, my lad!" But he could understand Dawson's uncertainty. "All right—you take the defense, I'll take the prosecution."

"Okay, sir."

Grant sat back. "First, the motive. We thought Otway had a strong one—but Ransley's would have been stronger. Otway might still have got something under a changed will, but Ransley could have been cut out altogether when Lumsden discovered he was going to marry a German—especially a German who was the daughter of an ex-Nazi judge. So he stood to lose a cool hundred thousand. What's more, there's the personal rift between him and Lumsden—which may have gone far deeper than he admitted. If he's fallen hard for Irma, he could have come to loathe his uncle. That would have made the killing easier."

Dawson nodded. "So far, I'm with you."

"Then we come to opportunity. To start with, the opportunity to get hold of Otway's prints for the frame-up. Ransley could have had that."

"He could have, sir. He'd have needed a bit of luck, of course. Otway didn't serve in the shop very often—and Ransley didn't go there very often. Strange, don't you think, if he happened to find Otway not only serving but holding a piece of glass that was about the right size for his purpose?"

"I wouldn't put it quite that way," Grant said. "Shall we say that he happened to find Otway holding a piece of glass, at a time when he was thinking of a possible frame-up? He'd then think—maybe I could use those fingerprints somehow. So he'd take the glass away —and then he'd have the idea of using the photograph frame. A bit of luck, maybe—but I don't see anything improbable about it."

"Well, perhaps not—if that's the way it was done."

"Then there were the circumstances on the night," Grant went on. "Ransley's cover story—pretty thin, eh? Pretending you've been hoaxed to explain an otherwise suspicious journey is a pretty old dodge, you'll agree. Knowledge of the domestic arrangements— we've seen that Ransley could easily have had that. . . . And, on present information, he could have had the opportunity to do the murder. We've only his say-so that he left his flat at seven. He could have left earlier and reached Radlett in time to watch Mrs. Bowen drive away. Then he could have gone in and done the murder and still have been at the hospital by seven thirty."

"He'd have been taking quite a risk, sir, with Otway supposedly due to arrive any time. He wouldn't have had much of a margin."

"He wouldn't have needed much, would he? The whole job needn't have taken more than about five minutes, if he'd gone with everything prepared."

"Suppose Otway had arrived early for once," Dawson said. "Ransley might have been caught in the act."

"He'd have heard the car draw up—and Otway's knock. And there's a back way out. He'd have had his escape route."

"True . . ." Dawson frowned. "Of course, sir, there's another risk he'd have been taking—the one that's actually tripped him up, as-suming he did it. . . . He couldn't have been absolutely *sure* that Otway would go to Lumsden's that night, could he? Otway might have been taken ill—had an accident—anything could have hap-pened. Whatever it was, Otway would have had an alibi, and the framework would have come unstuck—as it has—with Ransley as the only alternative suspect. Would he have deliberately accepted that risk?"

"Well—it's a point. But I'd say he probably would have done. After all, the prize was a fortune for life—and sudden illness or accident is a fairly outside chance. For that matter, so's a sudden cancellation by a regular visitor. I can see a greedy man weighing the odds—and still going ahead."

"He could have rung Otway—or his uncle—on some pretext, and checked."

"Not safely, if he was on cool terms with both of them—he'd only have drawn attention to himself."

"I suppose so. All right, sir, on with the prosecution."

"Well—there's this business of Ransley arriving at the hospital in a state of agitation. Now an intelligent man would know that he couldn't commit a murder and not be a little agitated a few minutes later. Not unless he was a hardened professional thug, which Ransley isn't. So Ransley very cleverly equipped himself with a reason—and, even more cleverly, didn't wait to be asked for it. He announced that he'd just seen a cat run over."

"Maybe he had, sir. It does happen. Bad night, too."

"A bit of a coincidence, don't you think?"

Dawson gave a reminiscent smile. "Remember that bloke George Endicott who drove into another car at Streatham—and found the driver was named George Endicott, no relation, a complete stranger?"

Grant nodded wryly. "I know coincidences do crop up—but I still don't like them. . . . Anyway, why should Ransley have told his girl about it—an hour after it had happened, and with the hoax to talk about—if he hadn't been building up his story?"

"If it was on his mind," Dawson said, "I reckon he would have told her. And while we're on it, sir, isn't Irma a point for the defense? Nice girl, I thought."

The inspector grunted. "Attractive, yes. Bright, too . . . I'm suspending judgment on the niceness. In any case, she wouldn't be the first nice girl to have got mixed up with a bad hat."

"Fair enough," Dawson said.

"Right . . . Now take another point—the signs of struggle . . . Ransley's a small man—he probably would have had a bit of a job dealing with Lumsden. It was a thing that worried me about Otway when we still suspected him—he could have squeezed the life out of Lumsden with one hand. At the same time, Ransley could have managed the job all right. He's a golfer—he probably has quite strong wrists. I'd say he fills the bill very well."

Dawson seemed less sure. "You could look at this in another way, sir—a way for the defense. Would a small man like Ransley really have chosen to *strangle* a man of almost his own size—even if the victim was old—with all the dangers of a struggle? Wouldn't he have been more likely to use a blunt instrument?"

"I don't know that he would," Grant said. "A strangler doesn't get blood on himself."

"Well, that's true. There's another thing, though, about this struggle. . . . If Ransley was framing Otway for the job, wouldn't he have wanted to minimize the struggle—knowing Otway's size? I agree he had to leave the photograph frame on the floor and the glass around—but wouldn't he have picked up the chair and put the telephone back?"

Grant considered. "You'd think so, wouldn't you? But he could easily have overlooked the point."

"You said he was intelligent, sir."

"I didn't say he was a superman. No one thinks of everything. . . ." Rather thoughtfully, Grant applied a light to his pipe. "Anyway, Sergeant, what have you got to say about Ransley's general behavior tonight? He was like a man on a hook—twisting and turning all over the place. I'll eat my hat if he really likes Otway. Did you notice he started by calling him Otway—then switched to George when I mentioned the possibility that he'd framed him? Remarkably sudden show of affection, I thought."

"It could have been nerves, sir. You grilled him pretty hard."

"Do nerves make a man with a clear conscience squirm and lie?"

"I reckon we've both seen it happen, sir. . . . A scared man . . . He'd have realized he was in a bad spot, innocent or guilty. He'd have known he was the obvious suspect, once Otway was in the clear—and you told him Otway had an alibi. Then there was the break with Lumsden, because of Irma. And worst of all, no explanation for being in Radlett that night except a hoax telephone call. In those circumstances, I think I'd have been on the defensive myself. And once you start that sort of thing, you get caught up. . . ."

"H'm . . ."

"Anyway, sir, isn't the fact that he behaved like a guilty man rather in his favor, in a sense? I mean, if he'd had the intelligence and nerve to do what we think he did, wouldn't he have put on a better show? Wouldn't he have been ready with a description of the voice that made the hoax call? Wouldn't he have referred to Otway as George all through? Wouldn't he have been all set to give a confident account of himself—instead of being muddled and evasive?"

"I don't know about that, Sergeant. I've seen several cool, tough killers suddenly go to pieces under cross-examination—and so have you. But it's damned hard to tell about behavior—I agree with you there."

Grant sat silent for a while, wondering about Ransley's true character. On the surface, the man didn't seem too well cast for the role of villain in the case. If anything was clear, it was that this murder had been plotted and executed by a man of strong nerve—a ruthless man—a gambler who was prepared to take big risks for a big reward. . . . Whereas Ransley had appeared to be just the opposite of that—a gentle, quiet man, a blood donor concerned with saving life, squeamish over the sufferings of a cat, flustered in a tight corner, nervous and sensitive. . . . But was that the real Ransley? He could have become a blood donor for the express purpose of showing himself in a good light if the murder became necessary. He could have invented the cat. His apparent nervousness and confusion under pressure could have been a skillful act—a screen to hide his toughness. How could one know, without an intimate knowledge of the man? And even intimates sometimes made mistakes. . . .

Still trying to see Ransley in the role, Grant switched his mind back to the facts of the murder night. The plan . . . As he recalled again the sequence of events, he was struck by a new aspect.

"Of course," he said, taking over Dawson's brief now, "it wasn't really a very sound frame-up plot—not if you examine it closely. . . . I don't mean in its details—we've already agreed some of those were weak—but in its general conception. Suppose Ransley *is* guilty—what was he expecting to happen after he left? Presumably that Otway would arrive at the house around seven thirty and find Lumsden dead. Then what was Otway supposed to do? Clear off and pretend he hadn't been there, because he knew he had a motive —and be caught by the fingerprints? An innocent man wouldn't be likely to do that—certainly no one could bank on it. The odds are overwhelming that Otway would have called the police and told them what he'd found. Of course, he'd still have been in a spot—he might have been suspected of doing the murder and then coolly reporting it as though someone else had done it—a sort of double bluff. . . . Though would it ever have seemed credible that a man with as strong a motive as Otway's would stick his neck out like that? Anyway, the real point is that the fingerprints would have lost their significance, because once he'd admitted he was there he could have said he'd fingered the glass after he'd discovered the murder —and no one could have proved he hadn't. So why go to all that trouble to frame him?"

"In fact," Dawson said, "it would really have been a good frame-up only if Ransley had known that Otway *wasn't* supposed to be there that night."

"Exactly—but then there'd have been the risk of an alibi. Whichever way you look at it, it wasn't basically a sound plan."

"The question is, sir, would Ransley have thought of all this?"

"Well, that's just it—we don't know."

There was a little pause.

"So what's the verdict?" Dawson asked, at last.

Grant shrugged. "Not proven, I'd say."

"My guess is he did it," Dawson said. "But there's not much solid evidence against him, is there?"

"Almost none, Sergeant . . . Certainly not enough to charge him."

"Where do we go from here, then, sir?"

"Well—we'll have to go on looking for something to clinch it—one way or the other. . . . Some way of catching him out . . . Of course, everything really turns on that hoax call. If Ransley invented it, then he's guilty."

"No doubt about that," Dawson agreed.

"And if he didn't invent it . . ." Grant suddenly broke off, frowning.

"What, sir?"

"Well, as we said, it would be a very odd chance if he'd been called to Radlett by a hoaxer on the very night his uncle was murdered there, without the two things being connected in any way. Too odd to believe in . . . If the call did take place, I'd say that someone was trying to make sure he'd be in the vicinity. Trying to frame *him,* in fact."

"That doesn't seem to make a lot of sense, sir—framing Otway with the fingerprints and Ransley with a hoax call."

"No, it doesn't," Grant said. "Not unless there's some third party concerned in this that we don't know about."

"Someone who had it in for both Otway *and* Ransley, you mean —and who also stood to gain by Lumsden's death."

"Something like that . . ." Grant didn't sound very taken with the notion. For a while, he sat toying with his pipe. "You know, Sergeant, this is a strange case. There's a sort of—calculated confusion about it. Almost from the beginning it looked as though it must be Otway or Ransley—but nothing adds up. . . ." Abruptly he broke off again. "I *wonder* . . ."

"What, sir?"

"Well, there's one thing we haven't considered yet, Sergeant. That the confusion's deliberate—and that Ransley and Otway are both in it together."

23

Dawson was cautiously interested. "You think that's possible, sir?"

"Well—let's take a look at it. . . ." Grant refilled his pipe and they began to explore the idea. "We know that it was in their common interest that Lumsden shouldn't change his old will. Now suppose they had a common understanding about it, too. A plan, carefully worked out, to get rid of him if he showed any sign of marrying again."

"Secret accomplices."

"That's right. In actual fact, a close relationship—in public, a front of complicated attitudes to each other, to get us thoroughly mixed up. Much better as a cover than simple hostility. . . ."

"They'd have had to meet pretty often to work out the plan," Dawson said, "and it's clear they haven't done that openly. . . .

Quite tricky—arranging a series of meetings on the quiet. Making sure nobody could possibly see them together."

"They'd have had to take a bit of care," Grant agreed, "but I'm sure they could have managed it. A rendezvous on a dark evening— a talk in one of their cars. Who'd have noticed them—or known they'd gone? I'm assuming now that Otway's wife would have been in it, too—with her background and tastes it's not hard to imagine —so they wouldn't have had to worry about her. And Ransley's more or less of a free agent."

"All right, sir—let's say they could have met. . . . So what would the plan have been?"

"Well, I'm just thinking aloud now," Grant said, "but maybe it was something like this. . . . Ransley would commit the murder, invent a hoax call to account for his movements, and frame Otway for the job by previous agreement. Otway would be safeguarded by his alibi. The frame-up would throw doubt on the alibi, at least to start with, and the alibi would throw doubt on the frame-up. That way, they'd argue, the maximum confusion would be caused, and it would be impossible to pin anything on either of them. Much safer than if one of them had attempted it on his own."

Dawson thought about it.

"Incidentally," Grant went on, "this would explain why Otway's alibi seemed so arranged. It *would* have been arranged—the phone call from Edinburgh fixed up beforehand, the report made to the supervisor to establish when the receiver was off. . . . With a frame-up in the offing, Otway would have needed pretty good proof that he couldn't have done it."

"He'd have got it more easily by taking his wife out to dinner at a restaurant," Dawson said.

"Ah, but that might have seemed *too* conclusive. As I see it, they'd have wanted a safe but not a simple alibi. Something rather tricky, to blur the picture a bit. Maybe to leave a faint uneasiness in the mind . . ."

Dawson slowly shook his head. "I'm afraid I can't see it, sir. Apart from anything else, it sounds to me like too poor a deal for Ransley. Whatever things looked like to start with, in the end the frame-up wouldn't have been intended to stick, and the alibi would have been. That's fine for Otway—but where's Ransley's safeguard? He'd have been left no better off than if he'd done the murder and framed Otway on his own. He'd be exactly as he is now, in fact—number-one suspect, and well up the creek. What would there have been in it for him?"

"Well, the plan would have given him Otway's cooperation," Grant said, "and that would have made everything a lot easier for him. He wouldn't have needed a lucky break to get hold of the fingerprints—Otway could have given them to him at one of their secret meetings. . . . He wouldn't have had to worry about timing, about the possibility of being caught on the job red-handed. . . . He could have had a telephoned all-clear from Otway about the arrangements for the evening—confirmation that Mrs. Bowen wasn't changing her visiting plans, for instance. He could have relied on Otway's sturdy backing after the murder, which in fact he's had. All those things would have made the job less hazardous."

"They wouldn't have made up for the one-sided arrangement, sir—Ransley doing all the dirty work for two. Look at the risks he'd have been running—a struggle with Lumsden that might have been more than he could cope with, an excellent chance of being caught if he made the slightest mistake, the certainty that he'd be suspected even if all went well—while Otway sat snugly at home, secure in his alibi, and no doubt ready to swear, if things had gone wrong, that he knew nothing whatever about it."

Grant gave a reluctant nod. "Yes—put like that, it certainly doesn't sound much of a deal for Ransley."

"As a matter of fact," Dawson said, "if there had been a joint plot I should think they'd have arranged that Otway would do the murder and Ransley would be framed. Otway's the big chap—he'd have had no physical difficulty. There'd have seemed a less strong case against Otway, too, because he was known as Lumsden's friend and protégé, whereas Ransley had a personal grudge. . . . And Ransley could have got himself an alibi just as easily."

"Maybe they couldn't think of a suitable way for Otway to frame Ransley."

"They could have worked out something if they'd wanted to," Dawson said with conviction. "Sorry, sir—it simply doesn't add up.

There's no evidence for it, and I can't see that it would have helped anyone. I reckon it's just not on."

Grant gave up. "I'm afraid I agree with you. Pity!—a lot of things in the case would have made more sense that way. . . . Well—it was an idea. . . ."

24

"So it's back to Ransley?" Dawson said.

"Looks like it, Sergeant." Grant tapped out his pipe. "We'll just have to hope our piece of solid evidence turns up."

"Like someone seeing his Consul parked at the end of Wilton Crescent at seven fifteen pip emma!"

Grant gave a tired smile. "Yes, I'd settle for that. In the meantime, as we seem to be deadlocked everywhere else, I think we might explore that other idea a bit further—a third party who could have had it in for both Ransley and Otway, and stood to gain from Lumsden's death. Just to cover the ground."

"There's no one else in the picture, sir. And no one else could have benefitted financially."

"There's still the chance of a personal motive," Grant said. "We haven't dug very deeply into Lumsden's life story yet."

"Would anyone else have had the necessary knowledge, sir—about the household, and so on? He'd have had to be someone who was pretty intimately acquainted with both Ransley and Otway, who was in a position to get hold of Otway's prints, who knew Ransley was a blood donor, who knew there was a photograph frame in the studio, who knew Otway visited on Sundays, who knew Mrs. Bowen went to her sister's. . . ."

Grant nodded. "I know it's asking a lot. I'm not sanguine."

"The only person who fills the bill at the moment is Mrs. Bowen herself."

"H'm . . . Well, as you said earlier, it certainly wasn't in her interest that the old boy should die. . . . But Lumsden had friends —supposed friends—and one of them might fit."

"What's the drill then, sir?"

"We'll get back to the studio first thing in the morning and finish going through Lumsden's papers. Then we'll start checking on his pals. . . . And maybe one of us should take a look at that cottage of his in Suffolk."

"Good," Dawson said. "I could do with a day by the sea."

25

There were some trying delays before they were able to resume work at the studio next day. First, Grant had to make an interim report on the case to the top brass at the Yard. Then he and Dawson spent a frustrating hour in Radlett tracking down a green car which someone had seen parked near Lumsden's house on Sunday night and had wrongly thought to be a Consul. When they finally reached Wilton Crescent, it was already eleven o'clock. A big furniture van was maneuvering by the drive, so they left their cars a few yards up the road and walked back. The house was shut up, but Grant still had Lumsden's key. The large studio, with only a single electric heater to warm it, seemed cold and dank, and the policemen kept their overcoats on as they settled down to work through the papers they'd not yet looked at. They concentrated now on noting the names of people with whom Lumsden had had social and professional deal-

ings—particularly names jotted down for appointments in his stock
of old notebooks. Otway, Grant thought, would probably know
who some of them were. . . .

After the thrusting inquiries of the previous day the job seemed
a tedious anticlimax and Grant had some difficulty in keeping his
mind on it. In the hard light of morning the possibility that some
unknown third party could have qualified for the murderer's role
seemed remote in the extreme. An unsuspected motive might well
be buried in these papers—but was it likely that anyone would have
gone to the trouble of framing both Otway *and* Ransley, when
framing one of them would have served his purpose just as well?
And how *could* any comparative stranger have acquired all that
detailed knowledge? Grant, mechanically noting names, found his
thoughts reverting constantly to Ransley, probing for some gap in
his story that would open the way to proof, weaving through the
tangle of the evidence. . . .

They had been at work for half an hour when the telephone
rang. It was the desk sergeant at the local police station—with dis-
concerting news.

"We've found the body of that tabby cat, sir. . . . In a ditch a
mile out of Radlett on the road from Barnet."

"Hell!" Grant said.

"You wanted it found, didn't you, sir?"

"Yes, of course . . . All right, Sergeant—thank you."

"Don't you want to see it, sir?" The policeman sounded slightly
aggrieved.

"No, thank you—just have it decently interred!" Grant hung up,
looking extremely exasperated. "Well—that's a setback I didn't
expect."

"Nor me," Dawson said.

For a while Grant sat in scowling thought. Then, slowly, his face
began to clear. "Of course, it's not decisive. . . ."

"It's quite a point in his favor, sir."

"Oh, it's that, all right. . . . But when you come to think of it,
it doesn't fundamentally alter the situation."

"It means he was telling the truth about one thing."

"Exactly—and that's all it does mean. . . . Look—suppose he

did do it. . . . He'd have known that he'd need something to explain his agitation afterward. But he couldn't have relied on a cat being run over. He'd have had to have some other explanation in his mind."

"Like what, sir?"

"Well, he could have intended to say he'd narrowly missed knocking someone down in the dark. A perfectly good reason for looking shaken, which no one could disprove. Then, on the way here, he happened to see a cat run over. And as it had actually occurred, it seemed a better reason. How's that?"

"It covers everything," Dawson said. He looked quite relieved. "Yes . . . In that case, we're really back where we were."

"Wherever that is!" Grant said ruefully. "Anyway, he's still in the running. . . ."

They returned to the chore of the papers—but not for long. Shortly before twelve, footsteps sounded on the gravel of the front drive. Grant finished the note he was making and got up to see who it was. As he did so, a key scraped in the lock of the front door.

Alert and suspicious, Grant stood listening. The front door closed. There were some shuffling sounds from the hall. Then the studio door opened and a woman came in. It was Eileen Marchant. She gave a gasp that was almost a cry as she saw that the room was occupied.

Grant said, "Hullo, Mrs. Marchant."

For a moment Eileen stood as though petrified, a plump hand pressed to her bosom. "Och, how you frightened me, Inspector! I hadn't a notion there was anyone here. I thought you'd all gone long ago. . . ."

Grant eyed her carefully. "What are you doing here?"

"Wait while I get my breath. . . ." Eileen flopped into a chair. Her appearance, Grant thought, was even more unkempt than on the first occasion he'd seen her. She looked like a rather jolly skivvy who'd just finished a hard morning's work.

"I've called to pack up the rest of Kathie's things," she said, after a moment. "The poor darling, she couldn't face coming back here after all that's happened—so she gave me her key and said would I do it for her. . . ."

"Ah—I see. . . . Well, that's all right. How is Mrs. Bowen?"

"She's a whole lot better today, thanks be to God. . . . She's been so poorly she hasn't been able to eat at all, not even the fine black grapes Mrs. Otway brought her, and there's been scarcely a word out of her all this time. But now this morning she's more like her normal self. . . ."

"I'm glad to hear it."

"You're not as glad as I am, Inspector, I can tell you, for we're short of room and it's more than I can manage with her needing to be looked after so much. Not that she isn't welcome to stay as long as she wants to, the poor thing, but it'll be better for everyone when she finds another job, which she's talking of doing. It'll take her mind off things and stop her brooding, which she does night and day, and anyway she needs the money, though it'll be different if Mr. Lumsden was serious. . . ."

Grant broke in on the flow. "What do you mean, Mrs. Marchant? Serious about what?"

"Why, about the money he was going to leave her. He told her last Saturday that he'd made a new will."

Grant stared at her. "A new will!"

"That's what he told her, and let's hope to God it's true. It was after she said she'd marry him, which is the right time for doing these things if a man's got feeling. . . . He said he'd jotted the will down while she was out shopping and got two fellows who were passing to witness it and then he'd put it away in a secret drawer. But she didn't quite know whether to believe him or not, because he was laughing about it—sort of teasing her. . . ."

"I see. . . . When did your sister tell you this, Mrs. Marchant?"

"It was when she came to visit us on Sunday evening that she mentioned it. Just a passing mention, that's all it was, for she's not a mercenary woman. . . ."

"H'm . . . I wish someone had told me."

"Well, we didn't give it another thought, Inspector, and that's the truth—not with this terrible murder, and Kathie being so upset. Not until today . . . It would be a wonderful comfort for her to know that he really meant what he said—and the way she looked after him, she certainly deserved something. . . ."

"Has your sister any idea where this secret drawer might be?"

"She has not. . . . That was the first she ever heard of it."

"What was she going to do about the will?"

"She was going to drop you a line," Eileen said, "and tell you about it and ask if you could help her, as you've been so kind."

Grant looked hard at her. "All right, Mrs. Marchant—you go and collect the things you want—and when you get home, tell Mrs. Bowen we'll have a good hunt for the will."

"She'll be grateful to you, Inspector," Eileen said. "I'll tell her for sure." She heaved herself out of the chair and went cheerfully off upstairs.

26

"Well, this is an unexpected twist," Grant said, as he closed the door behind her. "A most interesting development."

"It certainly is," Dawson agreed. "Especially if it turns out to be true!"

"Oh, I shouldn't think Lumsden would have told Mrs. Bowen he'd done it if he hadn't. It would have been a damned poor joke."

"She could have made it up, sir."

"Why would she do that?"

"To try and get something out of the heirs when the new will didn't show up? Sort of compassionate grant."

"M'm . . . It's possible—but I doubt it. . . ."

"You think Lumsden *would* have made a new will like that—off the cuff, and without a lawyer?"

"I don't see why not, Sergeant—in fact, I'd say it's just the sort of thing he might have done. . . . What was it Otway said about him—that he was impulsive and eccentric? That seems to cover it. Probably he enjoyed making the gesture. . . . Bit of a hypochondriac, too—and conscientious . . . Yes, it's all there. As for doing it without a lawyer, it was a Saturday, so he couldn't have got one. If he'd wanted to have the thing cut and dried right away, as a kind of engagement present, he'd have had to do it himself with whatever help he could get. . . ."

"That's true. . . . Why the secret drawer stuff, though?"

"Well, if there is a secret drawer, it would be quite a sensible place to keep a will. A bit of fun, too—like making a great mystery about a Christmas parcel. Harmless enjoyment of power . . ."

Dawson grunted.

"Personally I'm very much looking forward to seeing this document," Grant said. "It could give quite a new slant to the case. . . ." He moved around the studio, eyeing the old furniture. "I should think there could be a secret drawer in any one of these pieces. . . ."

He opened the Italian cabinet and inspected the inside of it, tentatively pressing various protruding pieces of the complex design as though he hoped to discover a concealed spring. "Fascinating bit of work."

Dawson prowled round the other antiques, in a desultory way. "It'll take some finding, sir. Reckon we'll need an expert on the job —someone who knows where to look."

Grant nodded. "I think you're right. What's the name of that sergeant at the Yard—the one who did the job for Armitage on the Chinese cabinet last year?"

"Thornton, sir."

"Ah, yes . . . Let's see if he's around."

Grant paused with his hand on the receiver as loud thumping sounds came from the room above. Eileen, trying to close a suitcase . . . When the noise had subsided he dialed the Yard and asked for Thornton. The sergeant was there, and replied at once. Grant explained his problem.

"Yes, I'll be glad to have a bash, sir," Thornton said. "But I'm tied up for a bit. . . . Just off to Luton on another job."

"When do you think you could do it?"

"Not before tomorrow morning, sir. As early as you like, then."

"M'm . . ." Grant looked at his watch. It was almost lunchtime. No doubt he could get an outside expert in from somewhere —but not, with any certainty, that day. "All right, Sergeant—I'll meet you here at ten o'clock tomorrow. Number five, Wilton Crescent, Radlett. . . . That's it. . . . Bye."

"Looks as though we'll have to be patient, eh?" Dawson said— and paused. "Unless, of course . . ."

"Unless what?"

"You don't think Ransley or Otway might know about the drawer, sir?"

"Well, I was wondering about that. . . ."

"In any case," Dawson said, "it would be interesting to have their reactions to the possibility of a new will. Especially Ransley's . . ."

"It would, wouldn't it? Okay—let's try. What's the Foreign Office number?"

Dawson looked it up, and Grant dialed. "I'd like to speak to Mr. Michael Ransley," he said. "This is Chief Inspector Grant. . . . No, I'm afraid I don't. . . ."

There was a little delay while the switchboard girl looked up the extension. Then a secretary came on the line. Grant gave his name again, patiently. Finally, Ransley spoke, "Hullo, Inspector . . ."

"I'm sorry to bother you at the office, Mr. Ransley," Grant said, "but I've got a piece of news that I'm sure will interest you. According to Mrs. Bowen, John Lumsden made a new will last Saturday. After she'd told him that she'd marry him."

There was a long moment of silence—so long that Grant said, "Are you there, Mr. Ransley?"

"Yes, I'm here. . . . That *is* interesting."

"Unfortunately," Grant said, "we haven't been able to find this will yet—apparently it was put in some secret drawer. Do you know anything about a secret drawer?"

"I'm afraid I don't. . . ."

"Ah . . . I thought perhaps your uncle might have shown it to you—in the days when you still used to visit him."

"No . . . Perhaps George Otway can help you."

"I'll ring him and see," Grant said. "Anyway, we're getting a man in tomorrow to go over the place with a fine comb—he'll find it if it's there. Thank you, Mr. Ransley."

"Have you—come to any conclusions about me?"

"Not yet, sir—you'll hear when I do. Oh, you might care to know that we found the body of the cat you mentioned."

"Well, that's something. . . ."

"Otherwise, inquiries are still going on. Good-bye, Mr. Ransley."

"Good-bye, Inspector . . ."

As Grant hung up, Dawson said, "Bit shaken, wasn't he?"

"I think he was, Sergeant."

"Not surprising, really, sir. The old boy could have left Mrs. Bowen a packet."

Grant nodded. "He *could* have left her everything."

"Then the murderer would have had all his trouble for nothing!"

"It's an intriguing thought," Grant said. "Right—now let's see if we can catch Otway before he goes to lunch."

He dialed the shop, gave his name, and waited. He was lucky. In a moment, Otway came on the phone. "Hullo, Inspector . . . How are things going?"

"Not much progress, I'm afraid," Grant said. "Nothing definite at all."

"You didn't get anywhere with your idea about Mike, I'm sure."

"Not very far . . . I'm not entirely satisfied with his account of his movements on Sunday night. . . ." Grant told Otway about the hoax call and the visit to the hospital.

"That's rather odd," Otway said.

"It is, isn't it?"

"Quite a coincidence . . . Still, if he said he was hoaxed, I'm sure he was. You didn't come across any real evidence?"

"No."

"And you won't, of course—I'm certain you're on a dud trail there. Anyway, Inspector, what's on your mind?"

"There's something I thought you might be able to help me with," Grant said. "Do you happen to know anything about a secret drawer at John Lumsden's house?"

"A secret drawer? No . . . Is there one?"

"According to Mrs. Bowen, there is—but she doesn't know where it is, either. . . . According to her, Lumsden made a new will last Saturday—and put it away in this drawer."

"Really?"

"So he told her. It sounds as though she may have become a beneficiary."

"It does, doesn't it? Well, good luck to her—she's certainly entitled to something. I don't suppose Mike and I will starve. By the way, Mike might know about the drawer."

"He doesn't—I've asked him."

"Oh . . . Well, I'm sorry I can't help you. I'm a bit surprised about the drawer—I'd have thought John would have mentioned it if there was one. . . . Anyway, I hope you find the will."

"We'll find it," Grant said. "We're having an expert in first thing tomorrow. . . . All right, Mr. Otway, thank you very much."

He put the receiver down and looked at Dawson. "Blanks all round . . ."

There was a bump in the hall. A moment later Eileen Marchant popped her head in at the studio door. She looked flushed with her efforts. "I've finished, Inspector," she said. "Will it be all right if I leave these things on the porch for my husband to pick up—then you won't have to be bothered again."

Grant went into the hall. There were two large suitcases with Kathie's initials on them, and two bundles. He looked at them, frowning a little.

"I don't think you'd better leave them outside," he said. "Someone else might pick them up. Look, if you like I'll have them dropped in at your house later on today. . . . Save you the trouble."

Eileen ran the back of her hand across her damp forehead, leaving a dirty streak. "That's very kind of you."

"Not at all—glad to be of service. You're sure you've got everything?"

"I've got everything that Kathie said."

"Good . . . By the way, may I have Mrs. Bowen's key now?—

I don't suppose she'll need it again. If she does, she'll know where to get hold of me."

Eileen looked slightly surprised—but she handed the key over.

"Thank you, Mrs. Marchant . . ." Grant smiled, but the smile didn't reach his eyes. "My regards to your sister."

27

Grant stood at the door, watching her till she was out of sight. Dawson, a little puzzled by the inspector's offer of baggage transport, moved the suitcases from around their feet.

"What's the idea, sir?" he asked, as Grant turned. "Think she may have swiped the Lumsden heirlooms?"

"No—not that . . ." With a slightly preoccupied air, Grant led the way back into the studio. "I thought it would give me an excuse for an informal call on the Marchant household later on, if it seemed necessary. . . ."

Dawson looked even more puzzled. "I'm afraid I don't get it, sir. . . ."

"There may be nothing to get," Grant said. "But this business of the new will does rather change the aspect of the case—and now I'm wondering about our Kathie. We've been assuming all the time that as she was going to marry Lumsden it was in her interests to keep him alive—and so it would have been as long as the old will was in force. But if he made a new will in her favor, that rather alters things."

"I can see that it might," Dawson agreed cautiously.

"It very well might. . . . Suppose, just for the sake of argument, that she preferred to have his money *without* marrying him. . . . I'm not saying she did, of course, not for a second—all I'm doing is considering the possibility. But we don't know much about her, do we? She could be exactly what she seems—a kindly, conscientious little woman who devoted herself to Lumsden, got genuinely fond of him, looked forward to being his wife and making his declining years happy—and may now find herself rewarded by being generously provided for in the new will he's just made. That's one possibility. . . ."

"It's the most likely one, I should think," Dawson said.

"Maybe it is—but there's an alternative. For all we know, she could be a clever, scheming adventuress. She's been in and out of a lot of jobs. She could have been looking all the time for an amenable rich victim. And with Lumsden, she might have found him. She could have come to him on the make a year ago, discovered he was wealthy, worked on him so that he fell for her, promised to marry him without ever meaning to, persuaded him to change his will in her favor—and then had no further use for him. . . . It's happened often enough before and I don't see how we can rule it out in her case. Marriage to an unprepossessing old boy like Lumsden wouldn't have been much of a prospect for her. She'd have been tied down, she'd probably have had to nurse him in failing health. It might not have gone on for more than a few years, but it could have seemed like a lifetime. She might well have preferred to enjoy his fortune without him. And she might have gone all out to do just that."

Dawson looked at his chief in astonishment. "You're not suggesting, sir, that *she* strangled him!"

"Well, hardly—she wouldn't have had the strength, that's obvious. . . . But there's such a thing as getting someone else to do a dirty job—in return for a share in the loot. Again, I'm merely toying with possibilities—but what about a relative? Say a brother-in-law?"

"Frank Marchant?"

"Why not? A big, tough, awkward-looking customer with strong hands, and all his thoughts locked up inside him? I wouldn't say he could be excluded—not on his appearance and behavior to date, anyway. . . . And the Marchants and Kathie are obviously a close-knit trio, or she wouldn't have gone popping over to Hendon every Sunday evening. For all we know, they could be a family of crooks. They could have had their plot in cold storage for some time, waiting for Kathie to bring off her ploy. And on Saturday she might have succeeded. Lumsden made the will—and on Sunday the bell tolled for him."

Dawson looked doubtfully at the inspector. "Are you serious about this, sir?"

"I'm putting it to you, Sergeant—that's all. Wouldn't you say it was worth looking into?"

Dawson considered. "Kathie would have had to be pretty sure what was in the will," he said after a moment, "to make it worth her while."

"I agree—but perhaps she *was* sure. . . . We don't know. We certainly don't have to accept Eileen Marchant's version of what happened, without checking. Kathie may have suggested what should go into the will. She may have dictated it. She may have seen it after it was made. She may know where Lumsden put it. She may even have sent her sister along today to collect it! We've no reliable information on any of these things."

"We know about her behavior after the murder, sir—and she was pretty upset over Lumsden's death. . . . At least, she seemed to be."

"My recollection is that she seemed dazed," Grant said. "And anyone can pretend to be dazed—especially if they've just seen the physical results of a strangling they've plotted. I should think it would come quite easy. I didn't notice any tears—did you?"

"No actual tears, sir . . . Sobbing noises."

"I could make sobbing noises right now, Sergeant, but it wouldn't mean I was brokenhearted! She could easily have been putting it on. She could have been malingering all this time—with sister Eileen's cooperation. Pretending to be too upset to think about the will—letting a decent interval go by before she started cashing in. . . ."

"She could have been," Dawson said. "But I certainly had the impression on Sunday that her feeling was genuine."

"You think she really liked Lumsden?" There was a note of challenge in the inspector's voice.

"Yes, I do. . . ."

Grant got to his feet. "Well—let's put it to the test, shall we? Here's Kathie, about to marry Lumsden, very fond of him. He's murdered—and she's naturally distracted. For a day or two she grieves for him. Then she gets her sister to collect her belongings from Lumsden's house. She tells her what to bring. She's going to look for a new job now—she can't bear ever to see the place again, because of its memories. This is her last contact with it. . . ." Grant opened the studio door and brought in the suitcases and the bundles. "I'm going to stick my neck right out, Sergeant. I'll make a bet with you—a small bet!—that there's not a single memento of the loved one in this luggage, not a single thing of purely sentimental value. Not a photograph of him, not a painting of his, not a letter—nothing!"

"I'll take you," Dawson said. "For a pint."

"Right . . ." Grant opened the first case and started carefully to unpack it. The contents consisted almost entirely of clothes. Very nice clothes, too, Grant noted. Dresses for every occasion. A luxurious fur stole. Two silk head scarves. Several pairs of good shoes. A wide selection of cosmetics of the best brands. A crocodile-skin writing case, with some old letters in it—none of them of any interest, none of them from Lumsden. Lots of oddments . . . Grant turned to the second case. More clothes. A jewelry box with several expensive-looking pieces inside—earrings, an antique necklace, a diamond bracelet. No sentiment there! A variety of personal belongings—all Kathie's . . .

"Try the bundles," Grant said.

Dawson opened them up. The smaller one had nothing but

soiled linen in it. The other was a jumble of minor possessions that Eileen had gathered up from various parts of the house. There was nothing whatever that related to Lumsden. . . .

Dawson sat back on his heels, his face puckered. "Well—you win, sir. Looks as though the old boy sank without trace."

Grant nodded. "Odd, don't you think?"

"It does seem a bit unfeeling. I'm surprised. . . . But it doesn't mean she'd have been prepared to murder him."

"It means, on the face of it, that she wouldn't have been deterred by affection."

"M'm . . . I still think it's most unlikely, sir."

"Well, let's consider it a bit further," Grant said. "We've already established that she could have had a motive. Now what about opportunity? We know that she and the Marchants were around at the time, because she was visiting them at Hendon—a quarter of an hour's drive away. So there'd have been no physical obstacle. Marchant could easily have slipped over and done the job. He'd have been known to Lumsden, by name, anyway, so he'd probably have been invited in—another point. As for creating the opportunity, you said yourself earlier that Kathie's the only person we know of, apart from Ransley and Otway, who'd have had the necessary knowledge of the household arrangements to work out the plot. How about that?"

For a moment, Dawson was silent. Then he said, "Now I come to think of it, sir, I'd say she had too much knowledge."

"Oh?"

"Yes . . . She would have known that Otway had cancelled his visit for that evening—which meant he could have had an alibi. So *she* wouldn't have made the mistake of trying to frame him."

"H'm—I see what you mean. . . ." Grant frowned. "Mind you, she'd probably have learned from Lumsden just how Otway was planning to spend the evening—staying at home, packing his bag, resting for his trip—with a very good chance that there'd be no one around except his wife. . . . There wouldn't have seemed much likelihood of a cast-iron alibi."

"I reckon the risk would still have been too great, sir. Anyway, if they decided to take the risk, why didn't they just frame Otway and leave it at that? Why bring Ransley into it? If they're guilty, Ransley isn't—and if he isn't, it means that the hoax call actually happened—with the probability that they were responsible for it. . . . You made the point yourself."

"Yes, I did. . . . Well, now, let's see. . . ."

Grant stood in thought for some time.

"How about this for a possibility?" he said at last. "Kathie, her sister, and her brother-in-law have planned to do the murder and share the proceeds. They know they'll be safer if they can pin the job onto someone else—and that person obviously had to be either Otway or Ransley. . . . In actual fact they've planned to frame Otway, and they've managed to get hold of his fingerprints. Then, at the last moment, he cancels his visit. They decide it isn't safe to rely on him any more because of the chance that someone may look in on him during the evening and that he may come up with an alibi. So they're left with Ransley. Now they can't frame Ransley directly, because they haven't got his prints—but they can frame him at one remove, by making the hoax call. *They* know Otway isn't coming, but they've no reason to suppose Ransley knows—and if he doesn't, it'll seem quite feasible that he should have attempted to frame Otway. . . . So they go ahead on those lines. . . . Kathie puts in the hoax call—maybe talking through a sock or something to disguise her voice, because Ransley's familiar with it. That could account for the bad line that Ransley mentioned. And now they're covered whatever happens. If Otway turns out not to have an alibi, as is very likely, he'll take the rap. If he does have one, they've got Ransley fixed up as a second-string suspect. How's that?"

Dawson grinned. "I reckon the criminal world's lost a mastermind in you, sir."

"Maybe . . . Well, what do you think?"

"Most ingenious . . . A lot too ingenious for those three, I'd say."

"How can you tell? Kathie struck me as being normally intelligent. Eileen's a chatterer, but she's certainly no fool. And Marchant's an engineer. He could have a brain like a computer."

"You said he was a *water* engineer, sir. He could be just a glorified plumber. Anyway, it all sounds much too complicated to me."

"Any solution of this case is going to be complicated, Sergeant—I'm sure of that."

"I dare say, sir—but this one just doesn't strike me as realistic. Look at the time factor, for one thing. It wasn't until Sunday afternoon that Otway told Lumsden he wasn't coming—and the hoax call was made around five. Could they really have thought up the new arrangements in a couple of hours? Worked it all out—arranged about the call—agreed what each had to do? There'd have been a heck of a lot of communicating involved."

"Well, the Marchants have a telephone, I suppose. And Kathie wasn't a prisoner—she could have slipped out to a public call box on the excuse of going for a walk. . . . Admittedly there'd have been quite a bit to discuss—but the main lines of the plot were already fixed. It would really only have been a question of getting Ransley to Radlett, once someone had the idea. I don't see any insuperable difficulty."

"It's all pure theory, of course," Dawson said. "There's no actual evidence at all."

"Not a shred . . . But then there isn't with Ransley—no hard evidence. And he's still high on our list."

"There's a far better case against Ransley than there is against Kathie, sir—even if we haven't found a way of bringing it home to him yet. . . . For one thing, we know that he was at the shop and could have got the glass and the prints with a bit of luck. We don't know that Kathie could."

"We can soon find out," Grant said. He looked at his watch. Otway would probably be eating now. "Let's go and have that pint you owe me. . . . Then I'll ring the shop again."

They spent nearly an hour over lunch at a local pub, without referring again to Grant's new theory. Most of the time they read the morning newspapers. As soon as they got back, the inspector phoned the shop. Otway was there.

"I'm sorry to keep on bothering you, Mr. Otway," Grant said, "but another matter has come up. Tell me—did Mrs. Bowen ever come to your shop?"

"Kathie? Oh, yes—quite often."

Grant glanced across at Dawson. "What did she come for?"

"Usually to buy paint and materials for John. Sometimes to bring one of his pictures—I displayed quite a bit of his stuff."

"When did she last come?"

"Oh . . . About three weeks ago, I suppose. . . . It's hard to remember—she was in and out so often. She used to fit in the visits with her shopping expeditions to the West End."

"Did you ever talk to her when she called?"

"Sometimes, yes . . ."

"And might she have seen you serving in the shop?"

"Well, yes . . . For heaven's sake, Inspector, you're not thinking . . . ?"

"I'm always thinking, Mr. Otway—though as you know it doesn't always get me anywhere! Thank you very much—that's all for the moment. . . ."

Grant put the phone down. "Well, there we are, Sergeant. Kathie could have got the prints as easily as Ransley—probably more easily, because she went oftener. . . . What's your view now?"

"I've an open mind," Dawson said. "In her favor!"

Grant smiled. "Ah, well—we'll see. I think I'd be remiss not to have another talk with her, anyway. And with the Marchants . . . Will you finish off Lumsden's papers—and I'll meet you at the Yard about five."

"Right, sir . . ." Dawson got up. "I'll help you out with Kathie's luggage."

28

Grant drove slowly to Hendon, planning his tactics as he went. Marchant would still be at work—which was probably just as well, since he might become awkward. Questioning the two women would be much easier without him. Kathie, first, because Grant had some testing matters to ask her about. Her real attitude to Lumsden, her health, the will . . . He would also want her version of how she and the Marchants had spent that Sunday evening—in detail. He'd see her on her own, of course. . . . Then Eileen, in the hope of turning up some inconsistencies. A single lie could be very helpful in these preliminary stages. Afterward, if the results seemed to justify it, an examination of Marchant . . . Possibly a check with the neighbors on any comings and goings during the evening . . . A look around the house for material evidence, too, if no one objected—the events of last Sunday could have left traces. . . . And,

all the time, an attempt to assess the capacity of these three people
to evolve the sort of complex, split-second-timed plot that someone
had managed to carry out. . . .

He reached Hendon just before half past three. Elmore Road,
where the Marchants lived, turned out to be a fairly typical bit of
North London suburbia. A few of its houses were detached and
rather bigger than the general run, but most were semis with identical fences and rectangles of garden and garages with concrete
drives. The only signs of life in the road were a group of women in
a conversational huddle around their prams and one or two people
walking in the crisp but pleasant sunshine. Grant had just slowed
to check the house numbers when he was struck by something
familiar about a woman approaching from the opposite direction—
a hatless, dark-haired woman in a fur coat. It was Kathie Bowen,
stepping out with a brisk click of heels—so well-groomed now, and
so attractively made up that Grant could scarcely believe it was
the same woman he'd seen at Lumsden's.

He pulled up alongside her and wound the window down.
"Good afternoon, Mrs. Bowen."

For a moment she seemed not to recognize him. Then she smiled.
"Hullo, Inspector . . ."

"Are you going somewhere," Grant asked, "or are you just out for
a walk?"

"Just for a walk."

"I've got your luggage in the trunk—I was bringing it over."

"Eileen told me you were going to. It's very kind of you."

Grant opened the door. "Come inside for a moment—it's
warmer. . . ."

Kathie got in. Her scent filled the car.

"How are you feeling now?" Grant asked.

"Much better, thank you."

"You certainly look much better. . . . Quite a striking recov-
ery!"

"Well, it's no good giving way, is it? You've got to keep going. . . ."

"That's very true. What does your doctor say about you?"

"He says I'll be all right now."

"You found a local man, did you?"

"Yes—my sister's doctor . . . Dr. Phillips . . . Young and very handsome!"   .

"I'm sure that helped. . . ." Grant made a mental note of the name. "Well, Mrs. Bowen, it's lucky we happened to meet, because I rather wanted to ask you a few more questions."

"Haven't you found out who did it yet?"

"Not yet."

"I thought you would have done by now. . . . What questions did you want to ask?"

"Well, I'd like to start with this new will your sister told me about. . . ."

"Oh, that . . ." Kathie looked troubled. "I didn't really want to say anything about it—not so soon. It seemed—well—grasping. . . . But Eileen said it ought to be found, if it's there. . . ."

"She was quite right, Mrs. Bowen. . . . Now when precisely did Mr. Lumsden tell you about it?"

"After I came back from the shops on Saturday afternoon. About four o'clock."

"What exactly did he say?"

"Not very much, really . . . We were talking about our wedding plans—he was in a very cheerful mood. . . . He suddenly said, out of the blue, that while I'd been away he'd made a new will and got two men who were passing to witness it."

"What did *you* say?"

"I said I didn't believe it. It seemed such an odd thing to have done, on the spur of the moment like that, and I thought he was just pulling my leg. But he said it was quite true. He said he wasn't going to tell me what was in it, though, and he'd put it away in a secret drawer where I wouldn't be able to get at it to look! He was in a very teasing mood. . . ."

"A man with a sense of humor, eh?"

"Yes, he was always joking. . . ."

"What happened then?"

Kathie gave a wry smile. "I said I wasn't interested."

"But you were, of course?"

"Well, naturally—anyone would be. I just didn't feel I wanted to talk about it—not then. . . ."

"This secret drawer he mentioned—I gather that didn't mean anything to you?"

"No, I'd never heard about any secret drawer."

"Do you think, now, that he actually *did* make this new will?"

"Oh, I think he probably did. . . ."

"Had he ever dropped any hint before about changing his will?"

"No."

"Did you expect that he would?"

"Well, I—I supposed he might after we were married. . . . I didn't really think about it."

"Did you ever think that you might marry him—before he asked you, I mean?"

Kathie gave the inspector a slightly amused look. "I won't say it never crossed my mind."

"He'd shown signs of being fond of you?"

"Oh, yes."

"Did your sister know about this?"

"Yes . . . I've always confided in her."

Grant nodded—and paused. "Well, it's been a great tragedy for you, Mrs. Bowen. . . . No doubt you'd grown very fond of Mr. Lumsden, too?"

"Yes, I had," Kathie said.

"What did you specially like about him?"

A rather vague look came over Kathie's face—a look that reminded Grant of Ransley, when asked about Otway. "Well, he was a very kind man—kind and generous. . . . An interesting man . . ."

"Did you have much in common?"

"We seemed to have—we always got on very well together."

"Did you admire him as a painter?"

"Yes—I thought he was very good."

"I'm told," Grant said, "that he often made a present of his paintings to his friends. Did he ever give you any?"

"One or two, that I specially liked."

"Did you ever sit for him?"

"Not for a painting. I did for some sketches."

"Which I'm sure you treasure."

"Of course . . ."

"I noticed from his passport, Mrs. Bowen, that he was in France in the autumn. Did you go with him?"

"No."

"Did he write to you?"

"Oh, yes . . ."

"Friendly letters?"

Kathie smirked. "Very friendly . . ."

"Well, at least you've not been left without mementos of him, have you? Paintings, sketches, letters . . . Perhaps you have a photograph of him, too?"

"Yes, I have. . . ."

Grant gave a little nod. He'd dug the pit deep, and was well satisfied. "Your sister told me you didn't intend to return to the house—very understandably. . . . So no doubt she collected these things for you. They're in your luggage, are they?'

Kathie looked at him with sudden uneasiness. "Why do you ask?"

"I'm just curious, Mrs. Bowen. . . . *Are* they?"

Kathie hesitated. "No—I gathered them all up and brought them away myself—on Monday."

"I see. . . . So they're at your sister's house?"

"Yes . . ."

Grant leaned forward and pressed the starter button. "Right— let's go and have a look at them, shall we. . . . You've no objection?"

"Why do you want to see them?"

"I want to find out if you've been telling the truth, Mrs. Bowen."

Kathie looked at him blankly. Then, slowly, she shook her head. "They're not at the house, Inspector."

Grant switched the engine off again. "They're still at Lumsden's, aren't they?"

"Yes . . ."

"You brought nothing of his away at all—and you didn't intend to. You're not grieving for him—you've already erased him from your life. You never really cared for him. Isn't that true?"

Kathie sat very still, looking straight ahead.

"Well?" Grant pressed her.

For a while she continued to sit in silence. Then, with a defiant shrug, she turned to him. "All right—I admit it. I *wasn't* fond of him—not in that way. How could I be? But I didn't dislike him as a person. We *did* get on well together. He *was* a kind man—and an interesting one. Rather a helpless man, too. He needed me. And I needed a home and security. It was a fair bargain."

"Did he know it was a bargain?"

"No—and he never would have done. I'd have made him very happy. I'm not ashamed of what I did—not a bit. . . ."

"Then why did you lie about bringing his things away? Why did you have to pretend?"

"I don't know—I . . ." She broke off. "I can't see what it has to do with you, anyway."

"Why did you pretend you were so upset on Sunday night?"

"I *was* upset. You don't have to be terribly fond of a man to be shocked by his murder. It was horrible."

The inspector grunted. "All right, Mrs. Bowen—we'll leave that for the moment. . . . Now, if you don't mind, I'd like to hear something of your background."

Kathie looked startled. "My background?"

"Yours, and your sister's."

"What do you want to know?"

"Where you were born, who your parents were, what you've been doing with yourselves all these years. Just in brief."

"All right," Kathie said, "though I can't think why you should be interested. . . . We were born in Donegal—and we were very poor. My father worked on the roads and gathered peat and we lived in a cabin. When I was nine my mother died and my father brought us to England. He got work in Norwich as a building laborer but he drank a lot and in the end it killed him. I was given a home by the English teacher in my school—she was a dear, I was very lucky—and Eileen went to live with some Irish friends of my father's, in London. When she was fifteen she started work—mostly serving in shops. In the end I went to London, too, and lived with

Eileen there, and worked as a shorthand typist. Then Eileen met Frank Marchant and married him, and after a bit I got married too—but I lost my husband a few weeks later. . . . I went on for a year or two with office work, but I wasn't any good at it and I didn't like it. So I got a job in a family, and I learned to be a house-keeper. I went to all sorts of places after that. I didn't keep the early jobs very long—but I gradually improved. . . . And I've been a housekeeper for someone ever since."

Grant nodded. "But you've managed to keep in pretty close touch with your sister, have you?"

"I've always tried to—though it depended where I was working. I've naturally seen more of her since I came to Radlett."

"How do you get on with her husband?"

"Very well."

"What sort of man is he?"

"He's all right. . . . I don't think he'll ever amount to much, but he knows his job and he brings home a regular wage and Eileen's fond of him."

"How did you get on with George Otway?"

"George? Oh, quite well . . . He was John's friend, of course."

"You don't sound too enthusiastic."

"Well, I did sometimes think he had too much influence over John."

"You found him a rival, in fact?"

"I wouldn't say that—but he *was* around a great deal."

"Who spoke to him when he telephoned last Sunday to say he couldn't visit—did you, or did Mr. Lumsden?"

"John did."

"Did Mr. Lumsden tell you what he'd said?"

"Yes, of course."

"Did you, by any chance, go out after that? Think carefully, please."

"I don't need to think. I went out to post some letters for John. . . . Why?"

"How long were you out?"

"About a quarter of an hour."

"In the evening, I recall, you left Radlett at seven. . . . You reached your sister's at about seven fifteen, I imagine?"

"About that."

"Was her husband there?"

"Yes."

"Did he stay there all the time you were there?"

Disquiet showed in Kathie's face again. "No—he went out. . . ."

"Where did he go? Do you know?"

Kathie hesitated.

"I shall check all this, Mrs. Bowen. . . . You'll gain nothing by holding information back."

"I'm not holding anything back," Kathie said. "It's just that . . . Well, as a matter of fact he went out in the Rover."

"Oh? Where to?"

"He didn't go anywhere special, as far as I know—he just went for a drive. He loves driving and he's never been able to afford a car of his own—all he's had is the Water Board car now and again. . . . Driving the Rover was a real treat for him, so when I was visiting I sometimes let him take it away for a little while. . . ."

"How long was he away last Sunday?"

"I don't remember exactly. About an hour."

"Just driving about, on a raw, misty night?"

"I don't suppose he noticed the weather."

"Possibly he had other things to think about?"

"I don't know what you mean," Kathie said. "I don't know what you're getting at, at all. . . ."

Grant leaned across and opened the near side door. "All right, Mrs. Bowen—you can finish your walk. . . ."

29

He drove the last few hundred yards to the Marchants' house with the feeling that he might be near the truth at last. It was possible to *see* this family, now, as a criminal trio engaged in a lucrative conspiracy. The ingredients were all there. . . . The background of deprivation, the hard struggle in early life, the yearning for security . . . Kathie, the better educated, the more sophisticated, the attractive, presentable sister, hawking her charms around until someone took the bait . . . Eileen, the energetic one, urging the others on, supplying the driving force . . . Marchant, the silent, sinister husband with the big hands, doing the actual killing . . . The three of them working out their murder plot in the quiet of this respectable suburb . . . Yes, it was possible. Grant had come across such ruthless family gangs before.

Well—now for the next step. Eileen must be closely questioned before Kathie got back. After that, Marchant. Where exactly had he been on this supposed joy ride? Where had he stopped, what had he seen? Grant would want that little outing reconstructed to the last detail. Meanwhile, there were the possibilities of the house itself. The murderer, whoever he was, had somewhere broken a sheet of glass for the frame-up—and disposed of the other sheet he'd brought away from Lumsden's. He might have been a shade too confident—he might have been careless about clearing up the debris. . . . It wouldn't be the first time that the contents of a dustbin had convicted a criminal.

Number 133 . . . Grant pulled up outside the gate. Looking at the house, he wondered why Eileen had complained of lack of room for Kathie. It was one of the larger, detached houses. It stood out from the rest not only by reason of its size, but because it badly needed a coat of paint and had a very neglected front garden.

Grant heaved Kathie's two suitcases out of the trunk, carried them up the path, and returned for the bundles. On his second trip he noted with satisfaction that the house was connected to the telephone. He knocked and waited. A slight frown settled on his face as a sound reached him that he hadn't expected. Through the peeling front door he could hear the pipe of a child's voice. In a moment there were footsteps and Eileen appeared. She was carrying a baby of about two, its mouth smeared with chocolate. She looked more untidy and disheveled than ever.

"Why, if it isn't the inspector!" she said. "And you've had to bring the things over yourself. Now isn't that a shame."

"It wasn't any trouble, Mrs. Marchant."

"Well, I hope not. . . . Kathie will be very pleased to have them. She's out for a stroll in the fresh air just now. . . ."

"I know—I met her."

"Did you, now. Well, will you come in, Inspector? You'll have to forgive the mess—I don't seem to have had a moment to tidy up today. . . ."

Grant said "Thank you," and picked up the suitcases. As he did so a large brown dog of uncertain breed came bounding out of the house and hurled itself at him, barking excitedly and clawing at the front of his coat. Eileen cried, "Will you stop it, Pat!" and hauled it off by its collar to some inner room, where it made resentful, snuffling noises behind the door. "He's a terrible dog," Eileen said, "I don't know why we have him."

Grant carried the luggage into the hall and set it down. "There you are. . . ." He looked around—and continued to look, with staring disbelief. It was a large hall, and could have been a pleasant one, but its walls were lined with furniture that plainly belonged elsewhere—not the least incongruous being a very large refrigerator. The space in the center, of bare, stained wood, was littered with toys and junk of every description. Two chubby little girls of perhaps four and five, with pink faces and mischievous eyes, were both trying to ride a tricycle at the same time. Through an open door, Grant glimpsed a sitting room in a similar state of confusion. Through another, he could see into the kitchen, where a mountain of unwashed crockery was stacked on the table and the draining boards. Adjoining the kitchen, part of a brick wall had been roughly hacked out, revealing an interior that looked to Grant like the boiler room of a very old steamer after an explosion.

"Got the workmen in, have you?" he said.

"We have not, Inspector—and more's the pity. . . . My husband has been putting in the central heating for the past twelve months and it's anybody's guess when the job will be finished. If it ever is, we'll have enough hot water for the whole street." She chuckled, as though it was all a great joke. "It's a bit awkward with the children sometimes—I'm scared for my life they'll hurt themselves on the rough bricks. But if it's not one thing, it's another. . . ."

Her flow of words was checked as the tricycle careered into her legs. "Easy there, you two!" she said, with an indulgent smile, setting the vehicle on its course again with her free hand. "They will get under your feet all the time. Well, now, will you not come into the sitting room?"

Grant took an indecisive step. "How many children have you got, Mrs. Marchant?"

"I have nine," Eileen said proudly.

"*Nine!*"

"I have, indeed. Six of them go to school, thanks be to God—though they'll be back any minute now. . . . Five girls and four boys . . . I wanted a football team myself, but you can't order these things, can you?"

Grant was staring at her. "Well—that really is a quiverful. You have been busy."

Eileen's eyes twinkled. "Och—the heat of the blanket takes away the toil of the day."

"Do you have any help?"

"And where would I be getting help from, Inspector? I just have to manage."

"Well—I'd never have believed it. . . ." Grant was having another mental picture now. Of the household in the evening. Of nine vigorous children, nine hungry mouths to feed, nine lusty voices raised—not to mention the dog's. Of noise and confusion. Of Eileen trying to cope . . . And of Frank Marchant . . . No wonder he hadn't finished his central heating! No wonder he was a silent man! No wonder he liked to slip out sometimes in a borrowed car! The sinister, plotting Marchant! Why, in such an atmosphere it would have been hard to organize a day trip to Clacton.

"Can I get you a cup of tea, Inspector?" Eileen asked.

Youthful voices sounded outside the house. Grant smiled and shook his head. "Thank you, Mrs. Marchant, but I ought to be getting along. I only dropped in for a moment to bring the cases. . . ."

He was still smiling as he squeezed past the throng of children at the gate. Ruefully . . . He felt a bit of an ass.

30

Dawson was waiting for him at the Yard. "Well, sir—how did it go?" There was an air of latent excitement about him that Grant attributed to eagerness for news.

"It didn't," Grant said. He reported his conversation with Kathie and described in pithy language the setup at Elmore Road and the crushing of his short-lived hopes. "They live in chaos—I've never seen anything quite like it. . . . If you can imagine the very opposite of a plotter's paradise, they've got it."

"I can, sir," Dawson said. "Must be murder when they're all at home!"

Grant scowled. *"Very* funny, Sergeant! Anyway, there we are. . . . Kathie was going to marry Lumsden for what she could get out of him and I'd say it's a bit on her conscience—but I'm sure that's the only thing that is. I didn't see Marchant, but I'd guess he's

144

quite inoffensive and just bogged down. And Eileen Marchant's a nice little woman in a sluttish sort of way—bit of a gypsy type, doesn't mind living in a dump—but cheerful, goodhearted, kind to the kids. I bet they all think she's a wonderful mum."

"Odd she should have a sister who's a professional housekeeper," Dawson said.

"I know—but that's the way things are in families, isn't it? They've obviously very different natures—and of course they had very different upbringings. . . . Though for that matter, I doubt if Kathie was all that good a housekeeper. The Radlett house looked a bit scruffy to me."

"She evidently suited Lumsden."

"Well, he was probably more interested in her than he was in her housekeeping."

Dawson nodded. "Anyway, sir, you couldn't say your trip was time wasted. You've eliminated an outside chance."

The inspector grunted. "Not one of my brightest efforts, I'm afraid. How have you been getting on?"

"I've finished the list of Lumsden's known contacts," Dawson told him. He passed a sheet of paper across the table. "I was just starting on the addresses."

Grant eyed the paper without enthusiasm.

"Mind you, sir," Dawson said, "I still think we'd do better to concentrate on Ransley."

"I wish we could, Sergeant—but how? He's told his story, and we can't disprove it. . . . He's only got to sit tight now, and he's all right."

"That's just it, sir. *Will* he sit tight?"

"What do you mean?"

"Well, I've been thinking about it while you've been away. . . . If he *is* guilty, I reckon he's practically bound to make a move now. Suppose *you'd* plotted a complicated murder, sir, to make sure of a whacking big legacy—risked your neck to carry it out—and then someone told you there was a new will in the dead man's house, which might mean you'd had all your trouble and danger for nothing. Wouldn't *you* do something?"

Grant frowned. "You mean Ransley might go to the house and look for it?"

"Well, he must know the house is empty, sir—and you told him our man wasn't going to start searching until tomorrow. In his place, I'm pretty sure I'd have a bash. He's only got to destroy that will and he's right back in the money again."

"Yes—but what about the secret drawer? Wouldn't that stop you?"

"I'd still have a crack at it, sir. If I didn't know where it was, I'd go along with an ax. I'd be pretty desperate. . . . Anyway, we don't know for certain that Lumsden didn't tell him about the drawer. We've only got his word for it."

"That's true," Grant said. "Well—it's certainly an idea."

"I reckon it's about our only chance of getting that solid evidence we need, sir. I know it's a long shot, but it seems worth trying. We've only got to catch him there and the case will be as good as over."

"Yes . . ." For a few moments, Grant sat thinking about it. Then he nodded. "All right, Sergeant . . . You've just talked yourself out of a good night's sleep!"

31

They had a quick meal in the canteen, packed a bag with food and flasks of coffee and flashlights, left word of their intentions, and at dusk set out once more for Radlett. Going so early, they knew, might well mean a long wait, but if their man was coming at all he could come at any time after dark and there was no sense in half doing the job.

They reached Wilton Crescent just before six and parked their cars near the hospital. Commuters were already beginning to trickle home from the city, so there was no reason why their walk to the house should attract any attention. But they went cautiously, and separately, alert for any watcher. The air was cool, but not frosty; the sky clear, but dark. They timed their arrival at the drive when no other pedestrian was passing, and slipped through the gate like shadows. Grant walked once round the house, making sure that all was quiet, that no one had preceded them. Then they let themselves in.

"Where's our base going to be, sir? In the studio?"

"I don't think so," Grant said. "If Ransley does come, we want to catch him actually looking for the will, if we can—and it's more likely to be in one of those antiques in the studio than anywhere else. . . . Let's see if we can find a good lookout point upstairs." He led the way to the second floor.

There was no upper room, it appeared, with windows commanding both the front and the back of the house. After a groping reconnaissance in the dark they settled for the main bedroom, which looked directly down over the front porch. Opposite the bedroom door, across a narrow landing, there was another room with a view over the back. By leaving both doors open they could shuttle conveniently and quietly between the two. The rooms, and the landing, were all close-carpeted, deadening sound. And when the moment came—if it did come—they could be down in the studio in a matter of seconds.

They arranged things for their comfort as best they could. Grant placed chairs on either side of the window, and Dawson dragged blankets from the bed to swathe over their coats. But, from the start, it was an unpleasant wait. They had no choice but to sit in total darkness. Because they were anxious not to miss the slightest sound, they had to leave the windows of both rooms open a fraction—and that, with open doors, meant a considerable draft. Even a shielded electric heater was out of the question, for fear the glow would show outside. Grant was taking no chances. . . .

At first, they walked around quite a bit. The movement helped to keep them warm, and lessened the monotony. One or other of them was constantly crossing to the back window and listening there. Ears, on this job, were going to be more important than eyes. Nothing much was visible from either window—only the lights of the houses around, and the vague loom of trees.

Their talk was desultory—and hardly at all about the case. The cold, as the hours passed, grew numbing, and neither of them felt inclined to any mental effort. At intervals they thawed themselves out with hot coffee and ate a little food. Grant longed to smoke his pipe, but decided against it. The scent of fresh tobacco in the air might be quite enough to arouse suspicion in a wary intruder. . . .

They amused themselves for a while by noting and identifying the great variety of sounds. . . . The hospital clock, chiming the slow quarters . . . Passing cars . . . An airplane . . . A bicycle. Music from a television set in one of the houses . . . Voices from next door . . . An occasional pedestrian . . . The clang of a dustbin lid . . . Running water . . . A dog yapping . . . The whistle of a distant train . . . Bird noises in the bushes . . . The stir of a faint wind . . .

But no sound of a murderer . . . Nine o'clock—and still nothing . . .

They speculated about their chances, for lack of anything better to do. "If he does come, sir," Dawson said, "what's your guess of the time he'll choose?"

Grant considered. "If it was me, I'd come around midnight. Late enough for the place to be getting quiet—early enough not to be conspicuous walking about in a suburb."

"Would you come on foot?"

"You bet!"

"Back way or front?"

"M'm . . . Front, I think. Less furtive."

"How do you rate the odds, sir?"

"If Ransley's guilty," Grant said, "I'd rate them pretty high. It was a perfectly sound idea of yours—I ought to have thought of it." He drew his blanket more closely around him. "Just bloody uncomfortable!"

"You're right, there. . . ." Dawson got up and slapped his arms across his chest several times. Then he looked out of the window. There were fewer lights showing in the houses opposite, now—a good sign. He crossed to the other room. He could sense, rather than see, the paved path, the shrubs that flanked it, the corner of the tool shed. . . . For a while, he stood listening. Then he returned to the bedroom and shared the last of the coffee with Grant. He felt fairly stoical about it all. This wasn't the first cold vigil they'd kept together—and no doubt it wouldn't be the last. . . .

32

All the same, by eleven thirty they were both growing pretty despondent. Sitting there in the darkness and the silence, it was hard to believe that anything would come out of their wait. They'd set a trap and they appeared to be stuck in it themselves—that was all. The road was quiet enough now—so why should Ransley delay? Almost certainly, Dawson thought, because he wasn't coming, because he was innocent. They were wasting their time. Wearily, the sergeant reckoned up the hours to dawn and blessed release. There were still a heck of a lot of them. If only it had been June, with sunrise at four! He crossed the landing again, and stared moodily out at nothing. . . .

A low call from the bedroom took him swiftly back to Grant's side. The inspector was standing with his ear close to the open slit of the window, listening. "I think there's someone out there, Sergeant." Dawson moved up beside him. Yes—he could hear something, too. Footsteps out on the pavement. They weren't exactly stealthy, but they were slow. Too slow for an ordinary pedestrian. Too slow even for a policeman on his beat. Tentative, cautious . . . The steps of a loiterer, with some plan in his mind. . . . They receded, faded completely, gradually returned—and stopped. There was a faint creak, as of a gate being opened. Then a crunch on the gravel . . .

"Blimey," Dawson murmured, "I believe we were right!"

The footsteps stopped again. Grant peered down through the window opening. He could see something—a moving patch in the darkness . . . A vague shape . . . On the lawn . . .

"He's walking on the grass," Grant said softly.

They waited, tense with excitement. The shape drew nearer. They could see, now, that the intruder was a *small* man. For a second the face turned upward, as though satisfying itself that no threatening chink of light showed at the upper windows. A pale face, with a high forehead . . .

"Ransley," Dawson said under his breath. "By God, we've done it, sir! We're home and dry!"

Grant was still peering down. He could see nothing now. The shape had moved away, out of sight.

"Probably looking for the best way in," he said. "I shouldn't think he'd have a key."

They stood motionless, listening for sounds of entry. The breaking of glass, the click of a catch, the movement of a window . . .

"He's taking his time," Dawson murmured, as the minutes passed in silence. "What the hell's he up to?" He crossed the landing and stood by the back window. Unidentifiable sounds reached him from below. They were so faint that they could almost have been imagination. . . . He waited impatiently for action, but none came. After a moment he returned to the bedroom.

Grant was looking out sideways through the slit of the window. "There's a light still showing in the house next door," he said. "I can see the glow. . . . Maybe he's lying low till they've gone to bed."

Dawson nodded in the darkness. If that was the explanation, it shouldn't be a long wait. Through the slit, he could hear a woman's voice calling a cat in.

The hospital clock struck twelve—an unwelcome interruption, masking other sounds. Then, as the last note died away, there were more faint noises at the back of the house. Footsteps again . . . This time both men crossed the landing. There was nothing to be seen below. It was impossible to tell what was going on. All Grant could make out was the loom of the shed. Then the darkness grew still darker. The slight glow from the next house was no longer there. . . .

"Light's gone out," Grant muttered. "Wait for it!"

The minutes passed. Still nothing happened. The tension in the upper room had become almost unbearable. . . . What was that? Footsteps again . . . Then, at last, the sound they'd been waiting for. . . . The sharp tinkle of breaking glass . . . The creak of a window being cautiously pushed open . . . A careful step on a hard floor . . .

Grant concentrated on his timing. They had only the landing and the short flight of stairs to cover. They could reach the studio in less time than a man could change his mind. Just a little more patience . . . They stood poised by the door, trying to read the sounds from below. A soft tread on carpet . . . A creaking board . . . A slight thump—unidentifiable . . . Confusing, that one . . . The studio door opening . . . Curtains being drawn across the studio windows—unmistakable . . . More footfalls . . . The click of a light switch . . .

Suddenly, incredibly, pandemonium broke out below. There were quick, heavy steps—a yell—the noise of something falling . . .

"Come on!" Grant cried, and rushed for the stairs, shining his flashlight ahead. Dawson pounded at his heels. They were down in a second. Grant threw the studio door open and burst in. Then, for a moment, he stopped dead. . . .

Michael Ransley was sprawled on the floor, flat on his back. Above him, both hands at his throat, was George Otway.

33

With a shout of "Break it up!" Grant leaped at the struggling pair. Dawson joined him, heaving at the collar of Otway's jacket. Together, they dragged the two men apart. Otway stood back, breathing hard, his face flushed, glaring down at Ransley. Ransley, hampered by the heavy overcoat he was wearing, got slowly to his knees, coughing and clutching his throat. Dawson helped him up.

Grant looked from one to the other, angry and baffled. He couldn't imagine how Otway had got there, or what he was supposed to be doing. The thought flashed into his mind that perhaps the two of them had been in a plot together after all—and that this was a case of thieves falling out. . . . "What the hell's going on?" he said.

Neither of them seemed capable of immediate speech. Otway was pointing accusingly at Ransley, his face convulsed with fury. Ransley was still gripped by paroxysms of coughing.

Grant's gaze swept the room. The cabinet was open. He stepped across to it and looked inside. A decorated flap was down, revealing a small drawer, half pulled out and now empty. On the carpet close by lay a sheet of folded paper and two fawn-colored slip-on gloves of soft leather. Grant picked up the paper, unfolded it, and ran his eye over the few lines of writing. "This is the last will and testament of me, John Edward Lumsden, of 5 Wilton Crescent, Radlett, in the County of Hertford, whereby I revoke all previous wills and testamentary dispositions. . . ." Grant read to the end, and put it carefully away in his pocket.

"Well," he said, in his most unpleasant tone, "if you two gentlemen have sufficiently recovered, maybe you'd oblige me by answering my question. What's going on? Who's going to talk first?"

"He was at the cabinet," Otway said. "Reading the will . . . When I came in and caught him he tried to rush past me. . . ."

"It's a lie. . . ." Ransley's voice was hardly more than a croak. "A damned lie . . ."

"Get him some water, Sergeant," Grant said. Dawson went off to the kitchen and returned with a jug and a glass. Ransley sipped the water, painfully.

"All right," Grant said, "we'll start with you, Mr. Otway. . . . Just what are you doing here?"

"What do you think I'm doing, Inspector? I came because I thought there was just a chance that *he* might come. . . . You'd told me you suspected him of killing John. I didn't want to believe it, as you know—but the doubt was there, because there seemed to be no one else. Then, this morning, when you said you'd told him about a possible new will, I suddenly saw a way I might test him. I thought that if he *had* killed John he might show up here tonight and try to find the will. So I got here early, and hid, and waited. I know it wasn't really my job, but I was sick and tired of having this thing hanging over us, and I thought maybe I could clear it up. And I was right. He came. . . ."

"What happened? What did he do?"

"He broke a window and climbed in. I gave him a few seconds and then followed him. I heard him moving about in here and I came after him. He was standing at the cabinet with those gloves on, holding the paper. You see, he *did* know where the secret drawer was. When he saw me he whipped off the gloves and dived for the door. He was trying to slip by me, but I grabbed him. He was like a wild animal, till I got him by the throat. . . . Then you arrived. . . ."

A sound escaped Ransley. Anger, disbelief, fear?—it was hard to tell. "It's not true, Inspector. . . . It's none of it true. . . ." His white face was contorted, his speech only just articulate.

"What's your version?" Grant asked.

"I was here first. I thought *he* might come. I was waiting for *him*. I saw him break the window and I followed him in. *He* was standing at the cabinet. *He* had the paper. *He* dropped the gloves. Then he attacked me. . . . I think he'd have killed me if you hadn't come. . . ."

Otway took a menacing step toward him, his hands clenched. "You're wrong—I was going to hand you over. But if I'd wrung your neck you'd have deserved it—by God, you'd have deserved it. . . . A man like John—your own flesh and blood! All for a bit of cash! How *could* you have done it?"

"I didn't. . . . *You* did!"

"He has an alibi, Mr. Ransley," Grant said.

"I don't care what he has. . . ."

"You're wasting your breath," Otway said. "You did it, and you might as well admit it."

Grant cut them short. "All right, that's enough. . . . We'll soon sort it out. . . . Mr. Ransley, what time did you get here?"

Ransley took another sip of water. "About half past eleven," he said.

Grant gave the faintest nod. "But if you thought, as you say, that Mr. Otway might come, and your plan was to arrive before him and watch him, why did you leave it until so late?"

"I didn't have the idea until late. I was on the point of going to bed. Then I suddenly thought of it."

"H'm . . . Well, describe your arrival. . . . Where did you come from, and what exactly did you do?"

"I left my car in a side road off the end of the Crescent and walked here. I went past the house, and back again, to make sure there was no one watching me. Then I came in through the front gate and crossed the lawn and went round to the back."

Again, Grant gave a slight confirmatory nod. "Then what did you do?"

"I waited."

"Where?"

"In the tool shed."

"The tool shed, eh? And what happened?"

"After about ten minutes I heard footsteps. They were coming up the path through the back garden. I looked out, and saw it was Otway. He went straight to the window and broke a pane of glass with a piece of wood. Then he climbed in—and I followed him."

"I see. . . . Well, just stay where you are—both of you. Watch them, Sergeant." Grant went through into the kitchen and let himself out of the back door. The tool shed was a little to the left, only a few yards from the broken window. He shone his flashlight on it. The door was open, swinging slightly in the breeze. He flashed his light on the floor inside. It was a wooden floor, covered with the dust of years—and the dust showed footmarks. The marks of small shoes. Rubber-heeled . . . He swiveled the light to the gravel below the window. A piece of wood lay there—the broken end of some tool . . .

He returned quickly to the studio. "I'd like to see the heel of one of your shoes, Mr. Ransley. . . ."

Ransley held up a foot. His heels were of rubber. Unmistakably, the marks had been made by him.

"Thank you," Grant said. He turned to Otway. "All right, Mr. Otway—now let's have your story in a bit more detail. . . . When did *you* get here?"

"Just before eight o'clock," Otway said.

"Eight o'clock, eh? That's rather odd. . . . The sergeant and I were here ourselves at that time. We were upstairs—listening to every sound. . . . We heard nothing."

"I came very quietly."

"You must have done. Which way did you come?"

"The back way."

"And you say you've been hanging around for Mr. Ransley ever since?"

"That's right, Inspector."

"Where did you wait?"

"In the bushes."

"What bushes?"

"There's a big clump of them to the right of the back door."

"And you were there for four hours?"

"Yes."

"That was quite a wait."

"You're telling me! But it proved to be worth while."

"H'm . . . Where's your overcoat?"

"My overcoat? Oh—I didn't bring one. . . ."

"Really? You came here for what might have been an all-night wait in the bushes, in late November—and you left your overcoat behind!"

"I don't feel the cold, Inspector."

"No doubt the bushes gave you some protection."

"I expect so."

"Would you care to show me these bushes?"

"By all means . . ."

"Right—lead the way. . . . You come, too, Mr. Ransley." They all trooped out to the back. Dawson kept close to Otway. Grant switched on his flashlight and shone it around. The garden to the right was flanked by rhododendron bushes.

"In there," Otway said.

Grant took a careful step or two, directing the flashlight beam ahead, probing among the bushes. "The ground's soft, Mr. Otway—it should show marks. . . . Especially if you were here for four hours. But I don't see any."

"I can't help that," Otway said. "I know I was somewhere around here."

"You should be able to point out the exact spot."

Otway peered among the bushes. "It's hard to remember. It *was* quite dark, you know."

The inspector gave a contemptuous grunt. "All right—we won't waste any more time. . . ." He led the way back into the studio. There he turned and faced Otway. "Well, I'm sorry, but I'm afraid I can't accept any part of your story. You didn't come here at eight o'clock, or we'd have heard you. You obviously didn't wait in the bushes. I think you arrived at a quarter to twelve, Mr. Otway—we heard some footsteps about then, but thought they were Mr. Ransley's. And *you* broke in—immediately. That's why you didn't trouble to bring an overcoat. You never intended to wait."

"You're quite wrong, Inspector. . . ."

Grant picked up one of the fawn gloves and held it out to Ransley. "Put this on."

Ransley slipped it over his hand. The fingers were a good quarter of an inch too long.

Grant took it back. "Now you, Mr. Otway."

"It doesn't mean anything," Otway said. "He probably got them large on purpose. He's framed me once already."

"Put it on!"

Otway did so. It might have been made for him.

"Fits like a glove!" Dawson said.

With a little relaxed sigh, Grant turned to Ransley. "All right, Mr. Ransley, you can go home."

"Home! But I . . ."

"Kindly do as you're told," Grant said. "You showed some courage in coming here, but you only complicated the situation. From now on, I'll handle things on my own, if you don't mind. . . . Go home and gargle! I'll be in touch with you."

Ransley hesitated—then shrugged his slim shoulders. "Very well, Inspector. Good night." He turned and went slowly out, his hand to his throat.

34

"Right," Grant said, as the front door closed, "let's make ourselves comfortable, shall we." He switched on both bars of the electric heater. "Pull up a chair, Sergeant. . . . You too, Mr. Otway. The night's young, and we've a lot of talking to do. . . ."

Otway sat down. His air of assurance had deserted him. His face was clouded.

Grant seemed in no hurry to start. He took out his pipe and filled it with slow care. In a preoccupied way he felt in various pockets for his matches. When he found them he lit up with great deliberation. Only when the pipe was drawing to his satisfaction— and the events of the night were beginning to fall into place—did he sit down too.

"Well, Mr. Otway," he said, "you seem to have lied yourself into a dead end, don't you?"

Otway didn't reply. He looked very uncomfortable.

"No one's ever going to believe your story, of course. You realize that?"

For a moment, Otway's silence continued. Then he appeared to come to a decision. "Yes, Inspector, I do realize it. . . . It was stupid of me to say what I did. I think I'd better tell you the truth."

"I think you had," Grant said. "Go ahead—I'm listening."

Otway's face took on a look of boyish candor. "Well, it was like this. . . . When you rang me about a secret drawer this morning, it honestly didn't mean a thing to me. I was rather busy and I didn't give it another thought all day—not, in fact, until after dinner. Then, when I was discussing it with Xanthe, I suddenly remembered something. John *had* once shown me a drawer in the cabinet that was worked by a knob. He hadn't called it a secret drawer, which I suppose was why it hadn't registered as that. . . . Anyway, there seemed no point in trying to get hold of you at that hour—I decided it would do just as well if I let you know about it first thing in the morning. . . . Well, Xanthe and I talked about the new will, and wondered what was in it—and especially what was in it for Kathie—and I suddenly thought, why shouldn't I go along and have a look and maybe give her a ring. I wouldn't be doing anyone any harm—and, after all, it did concern me too. Xanthe didn't much like the idea, but I thought it would be amusing and I felt like a run in the car anyway—so I drove up. It never occurred to me that anyone else would be here. I arrived just before twelve, as you said, and climbed in through the window, and found the will almost at once. Then, to my absolute astonishment, Ransley burst in. Before I could say a word he rushed at me and tried to grab the will—that was when I dropped it. He was beside himself. . . ."

"So you seized him by the throat," Grant said, "and tried to throttle the life out of him."

"I did nothing of the sort. . . . I told you, I was only holding him off."

"I happen to have eyes, Mr. Otway. Anyway, that's your amended story?"

"That's the truth, Inspector."

"All right—let's go into it a bit. If you felt you were perfectly justified in coming here to look at the will, why did you creep in by the back way?"

"Well, I—I knew I hadn't any actual *right* to be here, I suppose. . . . It seemed more discreet."

"Why did you wear gloves?"

"Oh—that was just habit. . . . I usually do wear them."

"Why did you lie about what happened?"

"That was wrong of me, Inspector, and I'm sorry about it. . . . I suppose I felt a bit ashamed. . . . Coming to look at the will, and then being caught here. Especially after I'd told you I didn't know about the drawer."

"Your lies involved Ransley. You accused him of things he hadn't done—things you'd done yourself. Weren't you ashamed of that?"

"No—because he killed John. I realized he must have done, the moment I saw him here. Everything suddenly fitted. He killed him, and then he heard about the new will and he came here to destroy it. Why should I care about him?"

"If he came to destroy the will, why do you suppose he was hanging about in the tool shed—as he undoubtedly was?"

"I don't know. . . . Maybe he meant to wait until the people next door were asleep."

"*You* didn't wait."

"I hadn't a murder to conceal. He was running bigger risks."

"He didn't seem to mind running risks. Wasn't it rather rash of him to go for you, as you say he did? A man half your size?"

"I told you, he was beside himself."

"What do you suppose his intention was?"

"To get the will . . ."

"He could hardly have destroyed it in your presence."

Otway frowned. "Well, *I* don't know—you'll have to ask him. If you get the chance, that is. . . . Frankly, Inspector, I can't imagine why you let him go—he'll probably be out of the country by morning. . . ."

"Are you quite sure, Mr. Otway, that you didn't come here to destroy the will yourself?"

Otway stared at him. "Good God!—as though I would. . . . I *wanted* Kathie to get a share. I was interested to see if I still figured in it, of course—that's only natural—but mainly I was concerned for Kathie. I was going to put the thing straight back, once I'd read it. . . ."

"*Did* you read it?"

"No—I didn't have time."

"Would you care to hear what's in it?"

"Very much."

"Then you shall. . . . Ten thousand pounds goes to you, and ten thousand pounds goes to Mr. Ransley. Mrs. Bowen gets the rest."

"I see. . . . Well, in the circumstances I'd call that very fair."

"In the circumstances," Grant said, "I'd call it more than fair as far as you're concerned. . . . But then I very much doubt if you're going to be free to enjoy your portion."

"What do you mean?"

"I mean that I don't accept your revised story either, Mr. Otway. You're glib and resourceful, and you did your best—but the story's obviously a tissue of lies from beginning to end. I don't believe you could possibly have overlooked knowledge of a secret drawer. If you had done so, quite innocently, and had remembered it later, I think you'd have made some effort to get in touch with me. I certainly don't believe you'd have gone to the trouble and risk of driving out here at midnight and breaking into the house just to *look* at a will that was going to be found in the morning anyway. And if you had just come to look at it I think you'd have said so right away when you were caught. Only a man with a deep sense of guilt would have invented the story you told. I believe that you came here to destroy the will, that Ransley found you on the point of doing so, and that you then attacked him."

Otway's face grew dark. "That's a very serious accusation, Inspector."

"It's not nearly as serious as the accusation I'm about to make, Mr. Otway."

"I don't understand you. . . ."

"You will very soon!" Grant applied a fresh light to his pipe and settled himself more comfortably in his chair. "This has been a very revealing night for me," he said. "What you might call the turning point in the Lumsden case . . . Quite suddenly, Mr. Otway, I'm seeing you in an entirely new light—and it's changed the whole aspect of the problem. . . ."

"Oh?"

"Yes, indeed . . . Up till now, you've seemed a rather decent fellow. . . . Genuinely fond of old Lumsden without being blind to his faults, grateful for his help, happy to give up your time to him, much more concerned about his welfare than his money. I was quite touched by your affection for him. I was impressed, too, by the frankness of your behavior since his death, by your courage when you came under temporary suspicion, by your reluctance to believe anything bad about Ransley, by your desire that Kathie should be provided for, even at your expense. . . . A thoroughly sound, honest, genuine chap—that was the picture."

"That's the true picture," Otway said, with a faint smirk.

Grant shook his head. "I'm afraid not. The true picture, I now see, is of a man who comes sneaking into an empty house in the middle of the night, with gloves on his hands so that he'll leave no traces, to make sure he isn't going to lose the fortune that he's worked for. . . . A grasping man, not an affectionate one . . . A man who lies about it when he's caught . . . A man who brazenly invents one unlikely story after another . . . A man who doesn't hesitate to shield himself by making untrue and damaging accusations against someone else . . . A man of ready violence . . . A man, in short, with the façade torn down . . . It's been a revelation. I see you now, Mr. Otway, not as a grateful and good-natured protégé, but as a dangerous crook without conscience or scruple. . . . And all because you came here tonight."

Otway sat very still. "All I can say, Inspector, is that you've got me entirely wrong. I agree that my coming could be misunderstood. . . ."

"There's no question of misunderstanding, Mr. Otway. I understand it perfectly. It squares with everything else. With your whole relationship to Lumsden . . . I ought to have realized, before, just what that relationship was. I had all the facts. You gave me most of them yourself, with disarming frankness. Here was Lumsden— a man who knew he wouldn't make his mark on anything, who knew in his heart he was a failure. . . . Unprepossessing and physically insignificant, aware of his inadequacy in the army, over-shadowed for years by a dominating wife, indebted to her for the wealth he wasn't capable of earning for himself, an indifferent painter rightly distrusting his talent . . . Neurotic and weak—not sure of himself over anything—isn't that what you said?"

"Well?"

"Then you came along. A robust, confident character, physically well-endowed, full of charm . . . The sort of man Lumsden would have liked to be—the sort of man he most wanted to be admired by. And you pretended to admire him. You bolstered his ego. You praised his work. You made it appear that you enjoyed his company. You visited him constantly. You played chess with him—and no doubt let him win. You made it clear that you regarded him as an esteemed and valued patron—and he loved it. At last he felt important. He made you a co-heir under his will—and, as you told me, got a kick out of letting you know. I don't doubt he also told you what he was worth—he'd have found the temptation irresistible. So there you were, with a snug hundred thousand pounds coming to you. . . . It's a classic case, Mr. Otway—of a clever confidence man working on the weaknesses of a rich patron for his own advantage."

"You have a powerful imagination, Inspector."

"It's been given a powerful stimulus tonight," Grant said. "Shall I go on?"

"If it amuses you."

"For a while, then, you were doing extremely well for yourself. You'd been able to get your hands on a little of Lumsden's capital —enough to set you up at the shop and give you an income. You were prepared to wait for the balance until he died. . . . Then, unfortunately for you, he suddenly showed signs of slipping through your fingers. He came under the influence of Mrs. Bowen. *She* pretended to admire him, too. *She* bolstered his morale. *She* gave him the friendly companionship he needed. He decided to marry her, as I'm sure he confided to you. You realized that the fortune you'd worked for was in danger—and that there was only one way to save it. By murder . . ."

"You know I didn't murder him," Otway said. "You know I couldn't have done. So why talk like this?"

"I'm going to forget your alibi for the moment, Mr. Otway. . . . I'm going to assume you *did* murder him."

"How can you forget an alibi? Besides, you know perfectly well that someone else tried to frame me. You must be crazy."

"Only the murderer would have tried to frame you," Grant said. "Only the murderer *could* have done. So if you're the murderer, *you must have framed yourself*. And that, I think, is exactly what happened. It's the only explanation that fits all the facts."

Otway stared at him. "What on earth would I do that for?"

"Oh, it makes perfectly good sense," Grant said. "Actually, it was a rather subtle and ingenious idea. As I see it, this is the way it went. . . . You knew that if Lumsden was murdered, both you and Ransley would be certain to come under suspicion, as his co-heirs— and that probably no one else would. . . . From the beginning, it would be between you and Ransley. You knew you could ride out the initial suspicion with the help of an alibi—but for ultimate safety, the blame had to be put squarely on the alternative suspect. It wouldn't matter if the case against him couldn't be *proved,* as long as the grave doubt remained. You had to provide grounds for that doubt. . . . Well, you couldn't frame Ransley directly and conclusively, because you hadn't got his fingerprints in a suitable form. But you'd got your own. So you framed yourself, knowing that as Ransley was the only other suspect it would be bound to look as though he'd framed you. . . ."

Otway's face showed reluctant admiration. "Well! Have you just thought that up this minute?"

"I wouldn't say that, Mr. Otway. . . . I've been living with the bits and pieces of this jigsaw for several days, you know. I've thought about nothing else. I've been trying all the time to work out a combination that satisfied me. . . . Tonight, the pieces happen to be falling into place—under the stimulus I just mentioned."

"Well, it's all absolute drivel, of course," Otway said, without heat. "How do you suggest I carried out this marvelous idea?"

"I'll tell you. . . . To begin with, you had to make sure that

Ransley would be in the vicinity on Sunday evening. You knew he was a blood donor—Lumsden would almost certainly have referred to it in the course of your many long conversations. You probably knew that he played golf on Sundays, and that he'd therefore be likely to return home at dusk for a bath and a change. So, late on Sunday afternoon, you arranged for a hoax call to be made to him, to get him to Stone Cross Hospital that evening. If he hadn't answered, no doubt you'd have postponed the plan until some other time—but he did. The call, I imagine, was made by your wife from your home. I hesitate to bring her into this, but I don't see how it can be avoided. I say it was probably made from your home because later you went out of your way to tell me that she dialed TIM— though you both had expensive watches and there was a grandfather clock in your sitting room that appeared to keep very good time. I assume you were covering yourselves in case I happened to examine your telephone account for that day. I'm not sure yet *why* the call was made from your home—but no doubt there was a reason, and it will probably emerge. . . ."

"This is wonderful," Otway said. "You really slay me, Inspector."

"Those could be prophetic words, Mr. Otway! Well, now, having made sure of Ransley, you drove to Radlett on Sunday evening. You weren't supposed to be there, of course—you'd already explained to Lumsden on the phone why you couldn't be. At one time, I wondered why you'd left the cancellation until so late—according to Whybrow, your trip to Edinburgh was discussed on Saturday and nothing had changed when you phoned Lumsden—but now I see. You wanted to make as certain as possible that Ransley wouldn't know about the cancellation—because if he had known he obviously wouldn't have tried to frame you that night. Not that there was much risk—you knew he was no longer in close touch with his uncle. Still, you wanted to minimize it. . . . All right, you drove to Radlett. Now what happened there? You parked your car in some quiet spot. You probably walked to the house and watched Mrs. Bowen leave—just to make sure the coast was clear. Then, I would think, you strolled along to the hospital and from a safe distance watched Ransley arrive in his car, which you knew well by sight. I'm only guessing about this, of course, but it would have been a reasonable precaution. Having satisfied yourself that the hoax had worked, you returned to the house and rang the bell. Lumsden let you in. No doubt he was surprised to see you—but you gave some explanation. You followed him into the studio—and strangled him."

Otway rubbed his hands together in mock appreciation. "A splendid reconstruction!"

"After that," Grant went on, unperturbed, "you set the scene. You'd brought along the glass with your fingerprints on it—glass which, you knew, Ransley would conceivably have been able to get hold of. You wanted the frame-up to be discovered, so you took care to see that it would be. You'd brought the wrong-sized glass— a nice clean sheet with no dust on the sides—and broken it in such a way that its substitution was bound to be discovered when your alibi was established and the inevitable check was made. You left the fingerprinted piece on the desk, because that was the only way to explain the prints. . . . When, later, you came under suspicion, and I gave you an opportunity to account for the prints—a loophole —you rejected it; again, because you wanted the frame-up to be exposed. . . . Before you left, you put the phone on its side and the receiver over the edge of the desk. There never seemed any good reason why Ransley should have left the phone like that—but you had to, for the sake of your alibi. It now appeared that a struggle had taken place—which suited you very well since Ransley was a small man—and to add to the impression you overturned a chair. You then departed with the original photograph glass—which, in view of your obvious attention to detail, I'm sure we shan't see again. . . ."

"Do go on," Otway said. "I'm fascinated."

"It's a fascinating plot, Mr. Otway. . . . Well, you left the house and returned to your car. It may be that you rang your wife and told her the job was done. I imagine you did, because while you were your way home she got in touch with the supervisor and reported that the Radlett number wasn't working. She did it from the house because you were anxious to give an impression of having been absolutely aboveboard. And you continued to give that impression. You played the part of a troubled innocent beautifully. A startled look here, a bit of indignation there, a spirited defense of Ransley, no real anxiety for yourself, grief that seemed genuine. And your wife backed you up splendidly, with that understandable touch of loyal anger on your behalf. You must have trained her well—or perhaps she has a natural aptitude? Anyway, neither of you put a foot wrong—until tonight. . . . And that, I think, just about covers everything."

"Except," Otway said, "the small point that I wasn't there! That I *have* got a complete alibi."

Grant knocked out his pipe. "I know, Mr. Otway. But this is one of the very rare occasions when I prefer to work backward. The argument runs as follows. You came here tonight to destroy Lumsden's will. Therefore, you're a crook. You nearly throttled Ransley, so you're a violent crook. In which case—taking all the other factors into consideration—the way everything fits you—you almost certainly murdered Lumsden. If you murdered him, you can't have an alibi. If you appear to have an alibi, it must be a fake. I don't say the logic's perfect, but I'm prepared to stake my career on the conclusion."

Otway gave him an arrogant stare. "That's just what you are doing. You'll be back on the beat, Inspector, if you don't watch out."

"I'll take that risk."

"You've not a shred of evidence. You've thought all this rigmarole up out of your head. And you know that I can bring witnesses. . . ." Otway looked into Grant's unwavering eyes, and shrugged. "Still, it's your affair. If you want to stick your neck out, go ahead. . . . Just try and *prove* that alibi's a fake—that's all."

"I'm going to," Grant said. "I don't know how, but I'm going to. . . . What you can fake, Mr. Otway, I can break."

With a simulated yawn, Otway got to his feet. "Well, this has been an interesting session, but I don't see any point in continuing it. I think I'll be moving along, if you don't mind."

"I do mind," Grant said.

Otway turned on him sharply. "I know my rights, Inspector. You've nothing against me. If I wanted to catch the first plane to South America, you couldn't stop me."

"I could—and I will. I'm holding you, Mr. Otway."

"On what charge?"

"Breaking and entering!" Grant said. "Come on, Sergeant, let's get him down to the lock-up."

35

They charged him at Radlett police station and left him in a cell, white with anger and threatening a defamation action as soon as he was free. There was an unveiled menace about him now that made Grant thankful he was securely behind bars. A formidable man, he thought, and now probably a desperate one. . . .

Before leaving the station, Grant rang up Xanthe Otway. He gave her the minimum of information about the night's events, and told her nothing of what was in his mind about the murder. Her husband, he said, had been caught breaking into Lumsden's house, had been arrested, and would be detained until he came up in court in the morning. Xanthe, after a moment of stunned silence, began to protest, to argue. . . . He'd only gone to look at a will, she said. Perhaps he oughtn't to have done, and he certainly oughtn't to have broken in, but it was a trivial matter really—it

169

wasn't like breaking into a stranger's house, and it was fantastic to have arrested him. Grant cut her short. She could come to the court in the morning if she wished. That was all he had to say. . . . As a precaution, he then rang the Yard and arranged for a man to be posted outside her flat, with instructions to keep an eye on her if she left.

In the quiet of his bedroom, an hour later, Grant applied his mind with zest to the solution of the final problem. The duel with Otway had stimulated him, driving away all tiredness. The challenge of the alibi was something he wanted to meet at once.

He felt no anxiety about the rightness of his judgment. He recalled how, from the very beginning, the alibi had seemed contrived. Now he *knew* it had been. Otway's insistence on punctual reports from Whybrow, the precise timing of the Edinburgh call, the establishment of the time of death by telephone receiver—all these were in place at last as calculated moves. The question was no longer "whether," but "how." . . . The problem had become a purely technical one. How had he done it?

Grant tried to imagine himself in Otway's position, at the time when the crime had been plotted. Otway must have faced the problem that *he* was now facing. How to be in Radlett, and take a telephone call at his house at the same time. Put like that, it seemed impossible. Yet by some illusion—some trick—it had been done. . . .

Grant concentrated on the telephone call. Clearly, it hadn't been a straightforward call. There had been something wrong about it, something unusual. But what? What had *seemed* unusual about it? Well, it had had one technically odd feature—and only one. . . . The operator had said that the line was good—and Whybrow said it wasn't. Curious, that difference of opinion. Curious, too, that the bad line theme had recurred. Ransley had said the hoax call line had been bad. *Echoing,* he'd said. Most peculiar . . . And suggestive . . .

Why had the lines been bad for some people, and not for others? Pure chance?—or had it been something to do with Otway? Some contrivance? Not a tape recorder, anyway—Grant had ruled that out, for reasons that still seemed valid. . . . Wire tapping? An impossible job for anyone who wasn't an expert—and not obviously relevant. Something else . . . Some sort of radio link? A V.H.F. transmitter in Radlett and receiver in Chelsea, working in with the phone call? Grant found it hard to imagine. . . . Too much equipment to move around and operate, too great a risk of interference and inaudibility . . . But a link of some kind . . . If Otway had spoken to Edinburgh from Radlett via his home, there must have been a link. . . .

A picture suddenly shot into Grant's mind. . . . Of Otway's sitting room—and Otway's study. Now *that* offered possibilities. . . . With his wife as his accomplice . . . And—*yes!* More recollections came surging in. Of Otway in the shop, that afternoon when Grant had called on him. Of Otway at his desk in the inner office. Grant had wondered about that at the time. . . . And there was the point that Otway had stayed late at the shop on the Saturday—and gone back there on the night of the murder—to get a catalogue, he'd said.

Yes—that *could* be it. . . . The method would have had to be well tested—but once tested, there'd have been no insuperable difficulties that Grant could see. The more he thought about it, the more it seemed to him that this was an explanation that fitted everything. He wondered if any marks could have been left.

He began to consider the idea in detail. The logistics . . . The time schedule . . . The various roles of the people involved . . . Soon he'd reached the point where he felt he could reconstruct the whole episode himself. . . . Which, of course, was exactly what he'd have to do. . . . Even if this method he'd thought of wasn't the right one, it would still discredit the alibi if he could make it work. And if it *was* the right one—well, that would open up much more dramatic possibilities. Enormous tension would be created by an accurate reconstruction—and someone might crack. . . .

Not Otway, Grant thought. A man who'd worked out and coolly executed an intricate murder plot, who'd killed a benefactor and framed someone else for it, who'd been caught in a compromising break-in and arrested and still had kept his head, would maintain a brassy front until the end. That was his profession. . . . But what about Xanthe? She must be a fairly tough baby, too, of course.

Hard, unscrupulous, greedy. . . . She'd married Otway, Grant re-called, about the time that Lumsden had made him his heir. Prob-ably for that reason. . . . She'd actively helped in the plot, she'd assisted in murder for gain without a qualm. A long-planned, cold-blooded, utterly ruthless murder. And she'd played her part after-ward with a composure equal to Otway's. . . . But that had been when all was going well. . . . The question was, how would she react to exposure, to the stress and ordeal of a demonstration of method, to the destruction of all her material hopes? To failure, and the prospect of a life sentence for murder, instead of the glittering future she'd been led to expect. Had she the guts to take that in her stride, without complaint? Was she really tough—or was she brittle? Well, tomorrow they would see. . . .

36

The next day proved to be one of the busiest and most exacting that Grant had ever known.

It began with a report to a hurriedly convened conference at the Yard; a consideration of the evidence by the higher-ups; and a green light to the inspector to go ahead with his plans.

Grant then drove to Radlett for the police court proceedings against Otway. In the box, he confined himself to describing briefly the break-in that had led to the arrest. Otway, who in spite of his overnight threats had taken no steps to obtain legal help, spoke up for himself with confidence. He explained his interest in the new will, and maintained that the break-in had been purely technical, since he'd always regarded himself as virtually a member of Lumsden's family and if he'd asked for it could certainly have had a key. Nevertheless, he admitted that his action had been ill-judged and

expressed his genuine regret for it. Police counsel then referred to
the likelihood of additional grave charges and asked for a remand
in custody for twenty-four hours—which was granted. Xanthe Otway
was present at the proceedings but was not permitted to see her
husband and subsequently returned to her flat, still under Yard
surveillance.

There, a little later, Grant telephoned her. He was not in a position, he told her at once, to discuss the case. He proposed to continue his inquiries at the flat that evening, and to bring one or two
people along there, including her husband. Had he her permission
to use the flat? If not, he would have to seek the necessary au-
thority. . . . Xanthe gave her permission.

Dawson, in the meantime, had been busy with several minor
matters and one major one. At an early hour he had remembered
to tell Sergeant Thornton that there was no longer any need to go
to Radlett as the secret drawer had been found. He had also spoken
to Mr. Forbes, Lumsden's lawyer, and reported the existence of the
new will. Afterward, he had driven to Otway's shop with another
officer, and the necessary warrant, and had removed certain bits
of evidence.

In the office, that afternoon, Grant and the sergeant experi-
mented with them. The tests were wholly satisfactory. Finally Grant
rang up Michael Ransley and brought him up to date with the
latest developments. "I'd be glad," he said, "if you could make it
convenient to come to Mr. Otway's flat at a quarter to seven this
evening. It may well be the end of the case."

"All right, I'll be there. . . ." Ransley paused. "I say, Inspector . . ."

"Yes?"

"Isn't this rather a bad line?"

"*Is* it?"

"Why, yes—it's . . ."

"Echoing?"

"Exactly."

"Thank you, Mr. Ransley. I'll see you this evening. . . ."

There were still a few more arrangements to be made. First, Grant
spoke to the telephone authorities and enlisted their help again.

Then he rang the C.I.D. in Edinburgh and held a briefing session on the phone with one of their sergeants. Finally he had another, easier session with a Yard man in the office, explaining his plan. And that was it. . . .

37

The Otways' flat had already filled up when Grant and Dawson arrived that evening. George Otway was there with his police escort, his face hostile and contemptuous. He had still, Grant noted, not troubled to bring a lawyer along with him. Xanthe Otway sat beside him, pale and silent. They were giving nothing away—and at this stage, Grant wouldn't have expected them to. Michael Ransley was waiting a little apart, looking like a man at once repelled and fascinated by the prospect of a public execution. A uniformed constable and a couple of detective sergeants stood by.

Grant put down the bag he was carrying and glanced at the grandfather clock. A check with his own watch showed that the clock was accurate to within half a minute. The time was ten minutes past seven. He stepped across to the study door, opened it wide, and left it open.

"All right," he said, addressing the assembly in general, but keeping a close eye on Xanthe, "let's begin. . . . We're here to re-enact some of the events which, I believe, took place last Sunday evening. As far as you're concerned, Mr. Otway, the chief difference is that tonight you're simply an onlooker. At this hour last Sunday, of course, you were in Radlett."

Xanthe looked sharply at the inspector, registering surprise. Otway merely shrugged. "You keep saying so, Inspector—but repetition doesn't make it true. . . . I was not."

Grant turned to Xanthe. He seemed almost clinically detached. "You, Mrs. Otway, were here in this room."

"Yes—with George."

"Alone! Tonight you'll be filling the same role that you filled on Sunday. . . . I have a man in Radlett to represent your husband. I have another man in Edinburgh to represent Mr. Whybrow. The telephone girl who put Mr. Whybrow's call through is also co-operating."

"Sheer foolery!" Otway said. "A stupid waste of everybody's time. . . . What are you up to, Inspector?"

"You don't know?"

"I haven't a clue."

Grant opened his bag. From it he took a pair of gray telephone receivers, linked by a coil of wire.

Xanthe looked at them—and looked away.

Grant held them out to Otway. "You've seen this piece of apparatus before, I think."

"I've seen something like it," Otway said.

"You've seen *this,* Mr. Otway. It was taken from your shop this afternoon—so I don't need to tell you how it works. . . . A simple intercom set, run by small batteries in the receivers, and quite efficient. . . . This set seems fairly new. Would you care to tell me when you installed it?"

"About three months ago."

"Ah, yes—quite recently. . . . Why did you need it?"

"I'd have thought that was obvious. So that I could talk to the shop from my office."

"I remember you used it when I was there. It struck me at the time as an unnecessary piece of equipment—an encumbrance rather than a help. But you had to install it, of course, whether it was suitable or not—to account for its purchase. What you really needed it for was to give you your alibi. You brought it home with you from the shop last Saturday evening, for that purpose. . . ."

"Nonsense. I don't know what you're talking about."

"No? Well, I'll demonstrate. . . ." Grant began to uncoil the wire. "First, though, we have a few minutes to wait. . . ."

Eyes swiveled to the grandfather clock. Its tick had suddenly become the noisiest thing in the room. Its hands stood at 7:24.

At 7:26 the telephone rang in Otway's study.

Grant motioned to Xanthe. "Your cue, Mrs. Otway. . . . Answer it as you did on Sunday."

"It didn't ring on Sunday. . . . It didn't happen. . . ."

"Answer it!"

She sat motionless. "Why—why should I?"

"If you've nothing to hide, Mrs. Otway, why *shouldn't* you? I'm asking for your cooperation."

She hesitated. Then, slowly, she got up and went into the study. Grant called after her, "Hold the receiver away from your ear, please—we all want to hear. . . ."

She picked up the phone. "Xanthe Otway speaking . . ."

A man's voice, clearly audible from the other end, said, "George here. . . . It's okay so far, Xanthe. . . . Kathie left on time—and Mike's just arrived at the hospital. . . ."

Grant gave a satisfied nod. "That was you, Mr. Otway, ringing from Radlett. We don't know precisely what you said, of course, but I imagine that could have been the substance of it. All right, Mrs. Otway, your turn to speak . . ."

It seemed to Grant that she swayed a little. "I tell you it didn't happen. I don't know what to say. I don't know what you expect me to say. . . ."

"Very well—in that case I'll have to stand in for you. . . ." Grant took the receiver from her and spoke into it. "All right, darling," he said. "Hold on. . . ."

Otway gave a loud hoot of laughter. In the tense atmosphere it sounded unreal, and it found no echo among the others.

Grant put the phone down on the desk, glanced at his watch, and went quickly to the intercom set. He picked up one of the gray receivers and took it back into the study. There, using pieces of cellulose adhesive tape, he joined the earpiece of the intercom receiver to the mouthpiece of the study phone, and the mouthpiece to the earpiece. Leaving the contraption on the desk, he left the study, trailing the wire behind him, picked up the second gray receiver, and took it across to the ivory phone in the sitting room, where he stood waiting. "Remember," he said, "Otway's still hanging on."

At 7:32, the sitting room phone rang. Grant paused for a second, then answered it. "Flaxman 0 0 six seven," he said.

A woman's voice spoke. "I have a transferred charge call for you from a Mr. Whybrow in Edinburgh. . . . Will you accept it?"

"Yes," Grant said, "put him through, please. . . ." He called loudly across the room—"George—it's Whybrow." Aside, to the tense audience, he said, "At the moment, the line is very good—as the operator said when I interviewed her." He picked up the second intercom receiver and quickly taped its earpiece to the mouthpiece of the ivory phone, and its mouthpiece to the earpiece. In a moment, faint sounds became audible—the muted sounds of two men talking to each other. . . . Grant stepped back.

"Naturally, we can't hear very much now," he said, "but we know what's happening. The police officer representing Mr. Whybrow is talking to the police officer representing Mr. Otway, in a perfectly normal way. One is in the Northern Hotel, Edinburgh—the other is in a public call box at the end of Wilton Crescent, Radlett. . . . On Sunday night Whybrow would have assumed, of course, that Otway was here. The man representing Whybrow is reporting on the sale pictures—and Otway is saying that he'll travel up on the night train. Understandably, Whybrow is finding the line not very good. It has an 'echoing' quality, eh, Mr. Ransley? That word of yours helped me quite a lot. I don't doubt, Mrs. Otway, that you used this instrument for your hoax call as well—to disguise your voice, which Mr. Ransley had once heard. That would also explain why you made the hoax call from home. . . ."

He paused. Faint murmurings were still coming from the taped receivers. He watched the clock. At 7:36, a tinkle came from one of the bells.

"That was Whybrow ringing off," he said. "Four minutes exactly . . ." He looked at Xanthe. "Are you sure you wouldn't care to take over, Mrs. Otway?"

Xanthe made no reply. Her face was ashen.

"All right," Grant said, "then I'm still standing in for you. . . . It's mainly a question of dismantling now. . . ." He untaped the sitting room intercom, hung up the ivory receiver, went through into the study, and untaped the second intercom. Finally, he spoke into the study receiver. "All clear here, darling! How was it?"

From the other end came the voice of the police officer representing Otway. "Okay, Xanthe . . . All right to go ahead?"

"Yes," Grant said.

"Then I'll get on with it. . . ." There was a little click on the line. Grant hung up the study receiver and began to coil up the intercom wire.

"Well—there you are, Mr. Otway. It may not have happened *exactly* like that—but it could have done, couldn't it? So much for your alibi! I imagine you and your wife must have practiced with this little toy quite a bit before you put your plan into operation— it certainly worked very smoothly that night. . . . When you were satisfied that you'd established your alibi—and only then, a characteristically wise precaution—you went and killed Lumsden. Afterward you drove back here, and later in the evening you went to the shop—not to get a catalogue, as you said, but to take the intercom set back and restore it to its place. Having first, of course, cleaned off the marks left by the tape . . . Unfortunately for you, you also scraped off some fragments of paint, as photographs at the Yard now show. And that, I think, takes care of just about everything. . . ."

Grant's voice became stern and formal. "George Otway, I now charge you with the murder of John Lumsden, and it is my duty to warn you that anything you say will be taken down and may be used in evidence. . . . Xanthe Otway, I charge you with being an accomplice in the murder of John Lumsden and I have to tell you that anything you say will be taken down . . ."

Xanthe turned wildly on Otway, her eyes glittering. "You *fool*, George. I told you you were being too clever."

"Thank you, Mrs. Otway," Grant said. "That was just what I needed to complete the case. . . . All right—take them away. . . ."

38

The flat quickly emptied of prisoners and escorts. In a few moments, Grant and Ransley were left alone. Grant put the intercom receivers back in his bag. Ransley picked up his overcoat. "Well—that was quite a demonstration, Inspector."

"You found it convincing?"

"Convincing—and very grim."

"M'm—I can't say I enjoyed it much myself. How's your throat, by the way?"

"Improving."

"I'm afraid this whole business has been a great ordeal for you."

"Yes," Ransley said.

"It was partly your own fault, of course. . . ."

"I know, Inspector—I was a fool to behave as I did at that interview. But at the time, I didn't see what else I could do. . . . It was

182

all because of Otway's alibi. When I first heard the details of the murder, I thought he might have done it. He seemed to be the only man besides myself with a motive—and I'd always distrusted him, always looked on him as quite unscrupulous. Then it appeared he couldn't have been there—which left *me* as the only suspect. And what a mess I was in! I knew you were bound to find out I'd been to the hospital—and I knew you wouldn't believe in the hoax call. I seemed to have no defense at all. I saw myself being arrested and charged, and Irma being involved through me in a ghastly, sordid case—and I thought at least I'd better not make things worse by admissions. When you virtually accused me of framing Otway, I just couldn't bring myself to say I loathed the sight of him. Any more than I could volunteer the truth about my relations with my uncle."

"What *did* you feel about your uncle—in general?"

"To be honest, Inspector, I hadn't any very strong feelings about him at all. I was rather sorry for him—he struck me as being a lonely, slightly pathetic man—until Kathie took him over. . . . I can't say I admired him at all—perhaps because in some ways I felt I was rather like him. I didn't enjoy being under a financial obligation to him—he made such a thing about it. But I certainly didn't dislike him—not until the Irma business. I couldn't face him after that—he was so terribly biased. . . ."

Grant gave an understanding nod. "Well, if you'll allow me to say so, Mr. Ransley, *I* thought she was a very nice girl. And if I were you I'd go straight along to her now and try to put this whole thing behind you."

Ransley smiled. "Thank you, Inspector. . . . I will."

39

Over a tankard of beer that evening, Sergeant Dawson summed up. "Well, I don't think much of them."

"Of whom?" Grant asked.

"Any of them. Otway and his wife—enough to give you nightmares for the rest of your life. Lumsden—halfway to being a case . . . Ransley—a bright boy at his job, no doubt, but I'd call him a bit of a twerp. Kathie—a middle-aged gold digger . . . What's she done to get all that dough?"

"More than you could!" Grant said.

"I dare say. . . . Anyhow, that's my view. I wouldn't say anyone comes out of this case very well, sir."

Grant gave him a complacent smile. "I think you and I come out of it *very* well, Sergeant. . . . Let's drink to each other."

Format by Mort Perry
Set in Intertype Baskerville
Composed by York Composition Company, Inc.
Printed by York Composition Company, Inc.
Bound by Haddon Craftsmen, Inc.
HARPER & ROW, PUBLISHERS, INCORPORATED

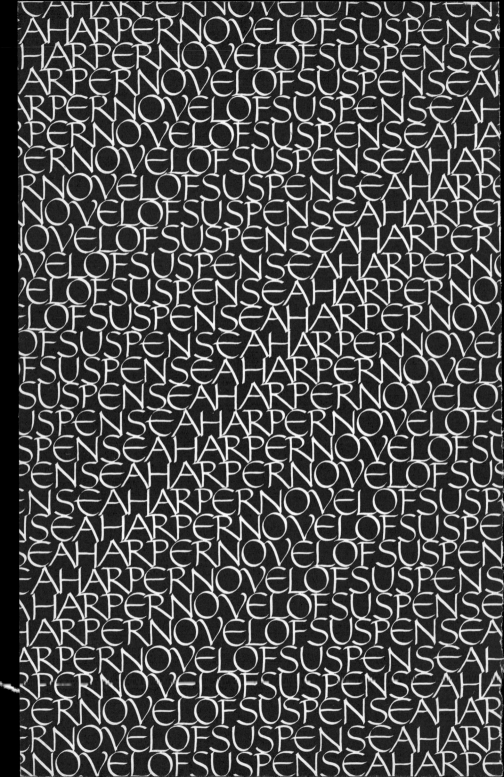